Love Bites Harder

(Book 2 of the Darkness & Light Duology)

By TL Clark

Explore the fae realm in safety!

 Happy Reading

Love & Light

TL xx

Published in the United Kingdom by:

Steamy Kettle Publishing

First published in electronic format in 2017,
and in print in 2018.

ISBN: 978-0-9956117-4-0

Acknowledgements

**Cover design by Robin Ludwig Design Inc.
www.gobookcoverdesign.com**

My deepest love and gratitude go to my husband.
Thank you for being so supportive and
understanding.

I also send massive thanks to my proof readers, beta
readers, bloggers, reviewers and
fellow authors who have shown tremendous
support.

And last but by no means least, thank you to all my
readers. Without you I am silent.

Table of Contents

The Story So Far

Maybe you read Love Bites (book 1) a while ago, and your memory is a little hazy.

Perhaps you've only bought this book without reading Love Bites; you're absolutely welcome to do that.

Either way, here's a little reminder, or introduction of the story so far.

However, if, unlike me, you have a great memory and just want to get stuck into the story, please feel free to skip to Chapter 1.

***

Shakira was always a bit of an outsider, and had never felt like she had fit in. She'd had an itch which couldn't be ignored any longer, so took the brave decision to move away from everything she'd ever known.

She found herself in a quiet Welsh village, just going wherever her car took her. She was strangely drawn to the location, and followed her instinct.

Shakira had been getting bad back pain, and uncharacteristically felt rough. It turned out that this was the forerunner of her transition. She'd had no idea that she wasn't human until that point.

Thankfully there was a friendly local witch named Cerys on hand to assist her.

Cerys helped her transform into her elinefae body, and explained what on Earth was going on.

Elinefae are a different species to humans. They have feline DNA running through them. Some strange humans took the tales of these blood drinking people and ran with it, creating the horror stories of vampires. Not that they like to be reminded of that.

They're not like those stories at all really. They're more like hippies living in a commune, attuned to nature. Yes, they hunt at night, have fangs, drink blood, are a bit pale, have fantastic reflexes and supreme hunting skills but that's as far as it goes.

The problem is that Shakira isn't even pure elinefae. She is also part sorceress.

This causes huge problems; elinefae do not allow any muddying of their gene pool waters. In fact, her own elinefae parents (the real ones, not the adopted human ones who brought her up) were executed for giving birth to her.

That clan thought Shakira had been killed too. But Lily, another lovely witch, had rescued her as an infant and handed her over to the humans, thinking that's where she belonged. She seemed human, and she hoped she'd be safe in their world. She'd taken her all the way from Scotland to Surrey via a portal, so she should have been safe enough.

But Shakira's instincts had brought her to her soul match, her mate, Pryderi (pronounced "pruh-DAIR-ee"). By the way, you'll find a handy name list at the back of the book.

It was love at first sight, and they instantly bonded. He gave Shakira her new name of Kiera (which is far easier for his kind to pronounce through their fangs).

But then her other genetic father (she technically has two), a sorcerer named Threaris discovered where she was. He needed her, or at least her blood to break his curse. He had bred her for this purpose. So he captured her.

Threaris had been a bad man. His true love (a witch named Azalea) had been killed in the time of battles by elinefae. He took this way too personally and set about killing the clans involved. That didn't reduce his grief, so he sought to kill more and more elinefae.

The elinefae obviously didn't take too kindly to this, and called in the help of a sorceress. Althea trapped Threaris in his own home, and had tasked him to seek amends.

But we're talking about an embittered male here, so he didn't take the hint. He spent years trying and failing to break his curse.

Frustrated, he managed to escape his prison for short periods, which was just long enough to meddle in elinefae life.

Threaris set two clans against each other. One clan was where Kiera's mother had come from, the other was her elinefae father's clan.

Kiera was reunited with Frydah, who was the faery enlisted to protect her in her youth. The faery had also been captured by the psychotic sorcerer, but helped teach Kiera how to use her magickal powers. And yes, natural/real magick is spelled with a 'k'.

There was also the offspring of a nereid at Threaris' home; Zondra. She'd been enslaved by the sorcerer, and was Kiera's allotted maid. Understandably upset by her imprisonment, and growing fond of Kiera, Zondra also helped the girl.

With their help, Kiera updated Threaris' curse, to try to get him to see the error of his ways. He was firmly stuck in place and now unable to harm anyone at all, thanks to the bracelet the three magickally created and Kiera's spell.

Kiera then travelled to the warring clans as soon as Cerys alerted her of their plight. Lives were lost, but she managed to stop any further damage, and Kiera brokered peace between her maternal and paternal clans. They were ever so grateful and she was welcomed by the Irish clan Leader, Ailene.

Bolstered by her success, Kiera went to Rhion, Pryderi's clan Leader in Wales. The pair sought permission to live together in their happy ever after.

But Rhion was not as impressed by Kiera's intervention. He blamed her for it starting in the first place, and feared the terrible power she could wield. Sorcerers were nothing but trouble as far as his experience had shown him.

He offered Pryderi an ultimatum; choose the clan he was sworn by blood oath to protect, or his mate and be forever exiled.

Phew! Is that enough action? It's quite a lot to take in if you've not read book 1. But that's the story so far in a nutshell.

The last book ended with…

Rhion declared, "You have a choice to make, Pryderi. Your mate or clan."

Pryderi was stunned. He couldn't seem to inhale. The wind had been knocked out of him.

Clan or his mate? Banishment or love? Either way his soul would be torn in two. Either way he would never be whole. He was doomed.

His sworn oath was to protect clan. It was a binding pledge he'd made as Watcher. To turn his back on that was unthinkable. But to live without Kiera was unimaginable.

There was a loud scraping noise as Kiera physically reeled back, taking the stool backwards with her. She saw the confusion on Pryderi's face. She also saw the very moment his choice was made.

He was not choosing her.

Chapter 1 - Devastation

Kiera was utterly devastated. She didn't need to hear Pryderi pronounce his declaration of betrayal. It was written across his face. Her heart was ripped in two, and her stomach was punched by an unseen force.

Vomit threatening to spew forth, she had to get away, and transported back to her cottage before her so-called mate uttered a word.

The place had remained vacant since she'd changed into the creature she now was, and her once cute home now felt alien. Her fingers ran along the countertop in the kitchen as she numbly filled the kettle to make a cup of tea, acting on auto pilot.

Her body was a mere shell. She had been filled with happiness and hope earlier today, having finally found the home where she truly belonged. But Rhion had shunned her, dismissed as an outcast, lucky to escape with her life.

She was more alone than ever. Now she'd lost the love of her life.

The kettle clicked off as it reached boiling point, bringing her attention back to the kitchen. She poured hot water over the teabag in her cup, turned to her fridge and took out the bottle of milk.

Her grunt of anguish echoed around the small kitchen. Of course the milk was off. She'd not been here in how long?

Angrily throwing the container into the bin, she sank to the floor, her back scarping against a cupboard. Her anguished grunt had opened the gateway to tears. The searing agony of separation scorched her from root to tip, the pain culminating in a ripping sensation in her stomach.

"How could he?" she cried out, clutching her middle.

'All that crap about being a soul match. I should've known it was complete and utter bollocks,' she thought bitterly.

Pryderi, her one true love she was meant to be tied to no matter what, had chosen his clan over her.

"Eurgh, fucking elinefae," she raged as her trail of tears grew larger and hotter on her cheeks.

Dropping her head and shoulders, she doubled over as pain drowned her. She screamed, shouted and sobbed until there was more of a Kiera shaped puddle than a humanoid on the kitchen floor.

Utterly consumed with grief, she didn't even notice the golden flash appear by her face. Neither did she hear the little gasp as the faery witnessed the scene of desolation before her.

Frydah had sensed Kiera's despair through their connection and tracked her down. She'd not expected to see this sorry sight. She wasn't going to be able to fix this on her own. She disappeared to seek help.

Kiera's body was wracked with sobs, her chest heaving as she tried to breathe through snotty tears. She was lying prostrate on the floor when the rapping noise of knocking on her front door caught her attention. But she couldn't move. She just hung onto the floor as if she would sink into a black hole without its presence.

Fortunately Cerys required no manual admittance. Receiving no response, the witch waggled her fingers at the lock which pinged open to allow her entrance.

"Oh Kiera," she exclaimed, running over to the soggy pile of girl on the floor.

Cerys sat on the floor and pulled the sobbing body over her lap and rubbed her back. An outright hug was out of the question with the girl in this state.

Frydah had re-emerged along with the witch, and hovered close by.

"He…chose…them…" Kiera wailed between sobs.

"Shh. Shh now. I can see it didn't go well. Time for explanations later. Come now, take a deep breath for me," Cerys soothed.

Kiera tried to comply, she really did, but her body was unwilling. She just wailed all the louder in her failed attempt.

"Oh my dear, this won't do. Calm yourself. Come on. We'll sort this."

"No…we…won't," Kiera bawled, "It's…useless."

"Now you stop that right now," Cerys instructed, pausing her rubbing motions.

"That's no way for a sorceress to talk." Her singsong Welsh accent softened the harshness of her words of tough love.

"To hell with...sorcery. What's the...point? It won't...bring him...back."

"Frydah, can you please make some tea?" Cerys asked.

"The milk...is...off," Kiera wailed, as if that was the worst thing about this situation.

The tiny golden being pointed to a cupboard, which opened to her magickal request. And two mugs floated down to the side.

Frydah flew over to Cerys' discarded bag on the floor and flitted around inside until she grabbed onto a bag of herbs and dragged them out. It was too heavy for her to lift up to the side, so she magicked the herbs into a teapot and willed the boiled water to pour over them.

With eyes bulging, and much gasping, Kiera was still trying to take deep breaths. Cerys smoothed the girl's hair, sending calming vibes over her.

Eventually, Kiera managed to stop crying enough to lift her head and let it flollop onto Cerys' shoulder. The witch encompassed Kiera in a cwtch, the most comforting kind of hug.

Once Kiera's breathing evened out, Cerys manoeuvred her so the girl's back leant against a cupboard. Pulling herself up, Cerys finished making the tea, and even found a thimble for Frydah's serving.

Carrying the cups through to the lounge, the witch also lit the open fire, helping the room feel cheerier.

Returning to the kitchen, she helped Kiera to her feet, and acted as a crutch as they made their way through to the fireside together.

Kiera's body plonked down heavily into an armchair. Curling her legs up with her feet to one side, she held her cup of tea close to her chest. The aroma of the herbs drifted up her nose, maintaining her fragile grasp on quietude.

Once Kiera sipped enough tea, Cerys ventured some tentative questions.

"So, what happened?"

"Rhion happened. That big, ugly, stupid, bigoted Leader won't allow me to live or set foot in his encampment," Kiera said, grunting.

"Oh, that ridiculous idiot."

"Yes. He told Pryderi it was clan or me. Guess which option the traitor chose," Kiera snapped out bitterly.

"The blood oath to protect clan," Cerys murmured dolefully.

"You should have seen him. It was embarrassing. He couldn't even look at me."

Kiera stopped what would've been a tirade of insults.

"Wait. Blood oath?"

Cerys drew herself eye level with Kiera and locked their gazes.

"Yes. Kiera, do not think for a moment this was easy for him. When someone becomes a Watcher they swear a blood oath to protect clan. It is binding in every sense of the word."

"But he could still have chosen me. Rhion offered him the choice. He chose them."

Cerys remained silent as she glanced down.

"And I thought humans were stupid," Frydah mumbled from the coffee table where she'd been sipping her tea quietly.

"Not helpful," Cerys admonished.

"Why does that big oaf think he has to complicate things?" Frydah asked, her hands on her hips.

Cerys rolled her eyes as she replied, "Because fear makes us all do stupid things."

They all finished their tea in silence. The air in the room felt stifling, as if Kiera had replaced oxygen with gloom.

"You need to rest," Cerys finally piped up.

Kiera could barely keep her eyes open, so she let Cerys lead her upstairs to the bedroom.

She was vaguely aware of hands removing her boots, and guiding her to the turned down covers. Sliding in between the sheets, Kiera's head dropped onto the soft pillow. Cerys smoothed Kiera's hair, pushing it out of her eyes, humming softly.

Closing her eyes, Kiera's mind drifted off along with the melody, and the soothing birdsong reaching her from outside. She was asleep before she knew it.

Cerys softly crept back down the carpeted stairs and dropped into an armchair, raking her hands over her face. Frydah's glow was dim and her beautiful golden wings hung limply down her back.

"Poor Kiera. So what now?" she asked, her wings twitching slightly.

"I wish I knew, Frydah. I wish I knew."

Chapter 2 – Impact

Pryderi was not fairing any better back at the elinefae encampment. Kiera's disappearance was sudden and akin to his arm being off him. He hadn't even had the chance to say goodbye.

Somehow, he had managed to bow to his Leader before running outside, into the trees. To anywhere that wasn't near anyone else.

He'd promptly thrown up in the undergrowth, pain ripping the fabric of his entire being. Yet he felt empty at the same time.

How could his Leader have forced him into this situation? For the first time in his life he felt hatred towards another elinefae, and it was aimed at his own Leader, who he'd always respected.

Upon accepting the role of Watcher, when he had pledged loyalty to the clan it was also to Rhion. He looked up to him, admired him.

Anger; he felt only anger and hatred. It boiled the blood in his veins. His lip curled as he hissed loud and long.

His duty was now to protect a clan he no longer wanted to be part of.

Pryderi only belonged with Kiera. The truth of his thoughts drove a knife through his stomach. He would have been sick again, but with nothing left, he was left dry retching.

His life was nothing. Not without her. He sank to the ground and flopped onto his back, vacantly staring up through the canopy of trees. Tears trickled down from his electric blue eyes to his pointy ears. He didn't care. He didn't even bother wiping them away.

"Hey hey, what is this, my friend?" Arwyn asked, stumbling across his friend.

"Not now, brother."

Arwyn's mouth gaped. *"What? What madness is this? I thought you would be busy in your den, but instead I felt a disturbance out here. Where is she?"*

"Home."

"Then why are you not with her?" Arwyn asked, his eyebrows scrunching together.

"Because I am a Watcher and she is a sorceress."

Arwyn paused. *"No. You do not mean..?"*

"Do not make me say it."

"Of course. I will not. He rejected her as a halfling? But this cannot be."

"It is," Pryderi replied with all the sadness of the world shining in his eyes.

"But you remained."

"I am oath bound to clan."

"But your soul is bound to her."

"So you feel my pain."

"I do. To be torn this way. My friend, my brother, I am sorry for this. But she stopped the battle. She is a proven hero and part sorceress."

"This counts for nothing."

"My brother, this feels truly wrong."

Arwyn squatted on the ground next to his friend. His clasped hands dropped between his open knees, his heels raised off the ground.

"Come, you can help me this shift," Arwyn offered, getting to his feet and stretching out his hand.

Pryderi wiped his arm across his forehead, groaned and slowly rolled to his feet, taking Arwyn's offered hand of support.

There was no fight left in him. He blankly followed his friend, allowing himself to be guided around the parameter lifelessly.

They had no further conversation. Pryderi thought he would completely break if he tried to explain any further, and yet he could think of nothing else.

His mind replayed all their happy moments. His fingers twitched as he remembered the feel of her skin under his hands, itching to feel her again. When he breathed in he did not smell the woodland he was in, but her scent. The yellow flowers of her signature, her natural aroma.

His feet fell on the forest floor, but he willed them to carry him to his mate. They remained stubbornly earth-bound though, taking him along his old path.

He was unresponsive to everything, even the rabbit which popped up as a potential prey fest.

At the end of the shift, Arwyn took Pryderi back to his den before seeking his own bed.

Sleep did not come easily. Pryderi was restless, tossing and turning as his blood rushed around his system, thundering in his ears.

When he did finally fall asleep, Pryderi's dreams were filled of Kiera, of their adventure and their union.

Pryderi did not turn up for duty the next morning. Arwyn was the first to rush to the elinefae's den. His heart was in his throat the whole way. Had his friend done the unthinkable? Had he ended his own life?

He cursed himself as he ran through the tunnel, bumping into others in his haste. He should not have left Pryderi alone, and should have called for assistance when he noticed how vacant his friend was. It was an unnatural state.

The door slammed as Arwyn hurried into the den.

"*Call for help*," Arwyn yelled frantically over his shoulder into the corridor as he rushed to Pryderi's cot.

Pryderi was curled up into a deathly pale ball, shaking and shivering all over. Sweat ran down his skin in rivulets.

Arwyn soaked a towel in the wash basin and applied it to Pryderi's head.

"Be still my brother. Help will soon be here."

"Is there anyone there?" he shouted over his shoulder again.

A shuffling of feet preceded the girl who appeared in the open doorway.

"Has someone gone for aid?"

"Yes. A call is being made to Cerys," the girl confirmed.

She gasped as she entered the room.

"What can I do?" she asked, wide-eyed.

"Cerys may be a while. Can you get me some herbs and hot water, Alana?"

The girl nodded bravely before dashing off to find the requested items.

Arwyn continued mopping Pryderi's brow. He wasn't even sure herbs would help, but he had to try something.

Alana returned within minutes, puffing with exertion. She had spilled some hot water in the process, but her hand was already healing from the scald.

"There is sage, rosemary and lavender in the water," she told him.

"My thanks," he nodded, taking the bowl.

Arwyn dipped the towel into the steaming, herby water and washed Pryderi's body with it. He brought the bowl close, hoping the steam would also help.

His efforts so far seemed to have no effect. Pryderi was still groaning and shivering. And panic was starting to take Arwyn into its grip. His jaw clenched as he kept watch.

It felt like a lifetime, but it was more like five minutes before Cerys came bustling into the room.

"*Go get Rhion. He needs to see this,*" she told Alana.

Arwyn had forgotten she was there, she'd been silent. The girl disappeared immediately, sprinting off to fetch her Leader at Cerys' command.

"This is what you get for tearing a matched pair apart," Cerys grumbled as she took over Pryderi's care.

"I already have my arnica tincture; the leopard's bane in my bag. But I need my bottle of opium extract. Can you also bring me some peppermint leaves?" she ordered Arwyn, dispatching him to her den.

Arwyn set off on shaky legs.

Cerys had put salt around Pryderi's cot, and was flicking the rosemary and lavender fronds from the water around the area, sending water droplets scattering. Pryderi had stopped groaning.

"Leopard's bane," Cerys explained, without looking up at Arwyn upon his return.

Reaching over, she grabbed the opium extract from his hand. Using the pipette, she dripped a few drops into Pryderi's mouth.

Arwyn span in mid-air as he snarled at the sound of a cough in the doorway.

Realising it was Rhion he should have stood down, yet he didn't stop snarling.

Cerys pretended not to notice as she carried on administering herbs and muttering chants.

Rhion strode into the room and eyeballed his insubordinate Watcher. Arwyn was immediately silenced, and meekly bowed, placing his fist at his heart centre.

Rhion brushed past him.

"Still think separating them was a good idea?" Cerys bitched at the Leader.

She was furious. She had always held Rhion in high esteem. This ridiculous decision was more fitting for Dougal, who at least had the excuse of being influenced by Threaris.

"It was necessary," he stated plainly.

"Necessary? Is that how you justify yourself? Necessary?"

"Cerys, you forget yourself. I am Leader of this clan. I must protect it."

"At all costs? And even if it was necessary, there are ways of doing things. Look at him."

"I will not remind you again, Cerys," he growled.

She looked up directly into Rhion's eyes, searching for any signs of bewitchment, but was disappointed not to find any. At least that would have excused his behaviour.

Rhion was acting totally out of character. It pained and shocked her to see it.

Turning away, she hid the tears which were welling up in her eyes. She wafted herbs and chanted as her mind dwelt on the greater problem at hand.

Yes, she'd been nervous initially about Kiera's heritage. But once she'd learned that the other half of her was from a sorcerer and not a human, she'd relaxed a little.

Ailene had welcomed Kiera amongst the Irish clan, had offered her hospitality and was grateful for her intervention in the battle. It had given her hope for the soul-matched pair.

Kiera had shown herself as nothing but good and pure. How could Rhion not see that?

Pryderi had stopped sweating, and his colour was slowly returning; what little colour he naturally had at least. Elinefae belonged to the night and lived in underground dens, so were naturally pale. Pryderi kept watch during daylight hours, so had slightly more of what elinefae would deem a tan than most.

His long black hair was sticky with sweat, and clung to his chiselled cheeks. He slowly opened his eyes. They too looked paler than normal.

"Welcome back," Cerys said softly as she held his hand and rubbed his lower arm.

He frowned.

"Cerys? Where's Kiera? Oh goddess, she's not here is she? She's gone," he began to rant and rave, clutching his hair in his fists.

Cerys swiped some more arnica tincture across his brow and stroked his hair away from his face. She hummed softly to her patient, who was quieted once more.

"*Arwyn, please can you get a tea made from those leaves?*" she asked, nodding at the peppermint leaves he was still holding.

The Watcher bowed and ducked out the room with a growl.

When he got back with the hot mint tea, he managed a weak smile, which Cerys returned. Rhion was no longer there. Arwyn sighed, his shoulders slumping.

"When he wakes up again please give him this tea. I need to go and check on Kiera, but I'll be as quick as I can," she told him, touching his upper arm.

Chapter 3 – Kiera Struggles

Cerys had used the portal system to travel to the elinefae encampment, and used it again now to travel home.

Taking a moment, she wandered back through her garden to enjoy the peace outside. Rhion had unnerved her even more than Pryderi's suffering. If Threaris wasn't safely locked away, banned from magick she would have suspected his involvement in all of this.

"Home sweet home," she announced with a sigh as she walked in.

"Home is where the heart is," a voice softly called to her.

Chen, the Chinese witch had managed to find his way back after many years spent apart. He had managed to find a way to stay this time, which gladdened Cerys.

She thought back to their own separation. Chen too had been forced to choose duty over love, as the clans battled and waged war in his home country. Her heart had been broken, and she'd spent too many years feeling lost and alone, trying to banish all thought of him.

She let herself get enfolded by his strong arms, her head rested on his shoulder as she sighed contentedly. If they could reunite she held the hope that Pryderi and Kiera would find their own way too. Although she added the wish for it to take far less time.

Chen and Cerys had been deeply in love, but it paled in comparison to that of a soul matched elinefae mated pair. Cerys physically shuddered how much worse it must be for Pryderi and Kiera.

The Chinese witch had remained at Cerys' house whilst she looked after her charges. He was not acquainted with the clan, and Kiera probably required female assistance from a friend.

"It's just so cruel," Cerys mumbled into Chen's shoulder.

"Rhion must have his reasons."

"Yes, but it seems to be fear. He is not a coward. It just makes no sense."

"Then we do not see the true reason. We will find it."

"Maybe, but right now I need to check on Kiera. Pryderi was in an awful state," she said, slowly pulling away.

"I will come with you. I am at your service," he told her as he smiled and bowed.

They strolled arm in arm to Kiera's cottage.

"Cooee, Frydah are you here?" Cerys called.

"And where else would I be?" Frydah grizzled.

"Oh, maybe checking on a certain sorcerer?"

"Relax. His butler is very attentive, and I've left Freddy in charge."

"Freddy?"

"He can be trusted. It's fine," she dismissed with a wave of her golden hand.

"How's Kiera?"

"Still sleeping like a baby."

Cerys sighed with relief, and tiptoed upstairs to check for herself, whilst Chen remained downstairs with the faery.

Kiera stirred, slowly starting to come to. Cerys sat on the edge of the bed and held her hand, aware this could be bad.

Stretching and yawning, Kiera slowly opened her green eyes. She frowned as she saw her witch friend there.

"Cerys?"

"I'm here."

"Where am I?"

"Back home in your cottage, dear," she said, rubbing the back of the girl's hand.

"Oh yeah. I remember. Pryderi is a poopeyhead," she stated sulkily, and pouted.

"Pryderi is a good elinefae."

"If he was so good he'd be here. He would have defended me," her voice started to rise along with her temper.

Cerys let her seethe. At least anger was better than what Pryderi was facing.

As she finished hurling insults, Kiera discovered tears starting to fall again.

"I don't hate him. I love him," she cried.

Cerys hugged her. "I know, dear. He loves you too."

"He does?" she snivelled.

"Oh, of course he does. Don't you begin doubting that. You should have seen him this morning."

"I would if I could," Kiera said, pulling away, looking down at the patch of duvet she was pinching.

"Sorry. Bad choice of words. He was suffering badly this morning."

"Good."

Cerys sat back in alarm. "Kiera! You take that back, young lady."

"Oh I don't mean it. I don't know what I mean," she cried, leaning in to retrieve her hug.

Cerys stroked the girl's back.

"Shh, dear. It's OK. We'll find a way. And he'll be fine. He's just feeling pain at the moment."

"He is? Like here?" she asked, pointing to her solar plexus chakra point.

"Is that where you feel pain?"

Kiera nodded and told her, "It's like there was something there, and it's been cut. Does that make sense?"

"Regrettably, yes. I think you managed to cut your etheric cord as you left."

"Is that why I can't feel him?"

"Yes, it would explain a lot, including his deep shock reaction."

"I didn't mean to."

"I know, dear. Here, let me apply this," she said, dropping some arnica ointment onto her finger.

She rubbed it onto Kiera's belly area. Kiera closed her eyes, and even managed a smile.

"Augh, that feels better. Thank you."

"I suppose we still have a lot to teach you."

"Oh no. I'm done. No more magick. It brings nothing but trouble," she declared, waving her hands.

"No more magick? Really?" Cerys gave one of her wry grins and held up the small mirror from her bag.

"Well, just as much as needed," Kiera huffed, seeing her 'normal' reflection shimmering back at her.

"Magick is part of who you are. And it is necessary if you're going to stay here." Cerys shuddered at the word necessary; it had become a swear word after her discussion with Rhion.

"I can't be with him if I have magick. Is there a way of taking it away? Permanently, not like I did with my father."

"Don't you ever say anything like that ever again," Cerys shouted, making Kiera jump.

"But it would mean I can be with Pryderi."

"Foolish bloody girl. I never thought I'd live to see the day you became stupid. You have a great gift. You are exceptional. Do you know what I'd give to have your abilities?" she yelled, waggling her finger.

"You're welcome to them. Take them," Kiera shouted back, throwing her arms in the air.

A cracking sound erupted as Kiera's cheek got slapped.

"You should be proud of who you are," Cerys yelled as she stormed out of the room.

"Yeah, I'm so proud to be the daughter of a psychotic sorcerer. It's just wonderful being rejected by everyone," Kiera called after her.

Chen grabbed Cerys' arm as she went to walk by him.

"What the hell just happened?" he asked, gawping.

"That girl has turned into a petulant child is what happened," she huffed.

"What is going on? This is not you."

"I'm not staying here. Please let me go," she said, squirming in his grasp.

"I will not. You need to stay here and resolve this."

Frydah vanished upstairs, and found Kiera still in bed, sobbing her heart out.

Kiera looked up with red puffy eyes.

"Are you OK?" Frydah asked, feeling worried.

"No, I'm bloody well not OK. Everybody hates me. I have no friends. Even my so called mate has rejected me," came the response amongst tears and sobs.

Frydah's drooped wings flicked as she quietly replied, "You've got me."

Kiera took a deep breath, and sighed out heavily. "You're right. I'm sorry, Frydah. I'm sorry. I'm a mess. My head hurts so badly I think it's going to explode. And now I've upset Cerys."

"You're a mess? Oh, I hadn't noticed," the cheeky faery mocked.

That earned her a half sigh half laugh.

"OK. But aren't I allowed to be? Argh, so much has happened. And just as I thought I was getting a glimmer of hope, a chance of happiness, it all got snatched away from me."

"Still thinking like a human," Frydah said with a sigh and shake of her head, "All things are transient. Besides, someone stole something from you, I say we steal it back."

"You have a plan?" Kiera asked, leaning forward.

"Not exactly. Not yet. But we'll find a way," Frydah confessed, pursing her lips.

"I hope so."

"I know so. Kiera, we've overcome worse already."

"Yeah, I suppose we have," she snivelled, "You're always on my side, aren't you?"

"What a funny question. Yes, of course I am. I always have been. It's why I chose you."

"What? Chose me? I thought Threaris asked you to look after me?"

Frydah raised her hand in front of her mouth as she giggled. "Yes, but who do you think gave him the idea?"

"No! You?"

"Mm hmm." Frydah nodded smugly. "Oh, I let him think it was all his doing, he is male after all. But I saw you first. You were so helpless and small. I felt your magick as soon as Lily brought you to your childhood home. That kind of magick is most unusual, and I just had to discover its source. Imagine my surprise when I saw a little baby, and one that was left with humans of all things.

"I stuck by you, watching you grow, protecting you. You were always so good. Not a bad bone in your body. I was curious, and worked a little magick to find out who your parents were. I found Threaris in his prison home, and the rest is history."

"You volunteered to be my guardian?"

"Uh huh." Frydah's golden glow brightened as she flitted up to hug Kiera's cheek.

"Thank you," Kiera beamed.

She tried to kiss the top of Frydah's head.

"Eww, no need to eat me," Frydah scoffed, but she was blushing wildly.

"You're like the best friend I never knew I had," Kiera said.

"Well, sometimes you knew about me."

"I don't know what to say."

"Nothing. You say nothing. Come on lazybones, time to get out of bed. We need breakfast. I'm starving," the faery instructed, tugging the edge of the duvet.

"You know, for a tiny being, your stomach is incredibly big."

"Look who's talking," she joked back.

"Help yourself to sugar in the kitchen," Kiera said, heading to the bathroom to have a quick shower.

Kiera dressed in her old clothes and maintained the glamour of her 'human' form. She couldn't very well wander around the village looking like her new elinefae self.

Chapter 4 – Foraging

"Well someone looks better," Cerys commented as Kiera walked into the lounge.

"I'm sorry," she whispered, grabbing Cerys into a bear hug.

"Well, better best forgotten."

Chen had been right. This wasn't her. There were too many things which just weren't right at the moment.

"I need food," Kiera declared.

"You can show your face at the café," Cerys told her.

"Right. I suppose I need to start working there again now. I need to pay my way."

"Just remember, you've been poorly with the flu."

"Of course."

Kiera's shoulders slumped at the thought of returning to her old life. Her eyes had been opened to a whole new world. Could she really do this? Live as if she'd never seen all those things?

She decided it was the best option. She couldn't be with Pryderi. Going to Ireland to live with Ailene's clan didn't feel right; she didn't want to be around elinefae without her mate. And the thought of returning to the prison of her father's home made her stomach churn.

"Err, it is still Sunday," Chen hesitantly interjected.

"Oh bloody hell. Yes, fine. We'll go to the pub. They'll be open, at least," Cerys acknowledged.

"No objections here," Kiera said, welcoming the thought of not having to face Annie just yet.

She took a deep breath, and collected her bag on her way out. Cerys and Chen accompanied her, whilst Frydah sat happily on a mountain of sugar in the kitchen.

They managed to order an all-day breakfast each, and sat at a table in a quiet corner. Kiera felt guilty. She had recently been in this pub, making new friends, enjoying a lovely lunch like a normal person. But now she wasn't that person any more. She wasn't even human. It felt wrong to be here.

She stabbed at her food, pondering her future. Was this it? Was she going to have to live the rest of her life in a lie, hiding who she truly was?

"How do you do it?" she asked Cerys in a hushed tone.

"Do what, dear?"

"Live amongst these people?"

"Oh, it's not so bad really. Of course, I don't have to err, change my appearance to fit in. Running a metaphysical store, people expect me to be a little weird," she explained quietly.

"But I do. I feel like I'm lying."

"And women never wear makeup? Is that not just a sort of mask to hide behind? Yours is just a little more elaborate."

"I suppose."

"You were fine here before. You were happy enough."

"I thought I was."

"You were. You can be again."

"Were you?" Kiera asked, emphasising the 'you'.

"Kiera, I was content. Was I over the moon happy? No. But I did alright. And I'm happy now."

"I don't know if I can do this," she said, wincing.

"Of course you can. You'll be fine, my dear. And I'll be here to help."

They finished their meal in silence. Kiera had lost her appetite and didn't eat much at all.

When it came down to it, Kiera just didn't know if she wanted to be alright with this life. It felt wrong, like badly fitting clothes.

Walking out of the pub together, Cerys was trying to plan for the immediate future. Kiera blinked through the rain and let the bird song soak into her soul.

"Chen, can you take Kiera home, please? I'll just pop to my house and collect a few supplies."

"Of course," he said, taking Kiera's elbow.

The poor girl looked as if she could barely stand.

"Uh huh," Cerys cautioned, feeling the magickal build up from Kiera.

"Oh, but I don't want to walk," Kiera moaned, feeling frustrated at being held back from transporting herself.

"It is just one of those things, I'm afraid."

Kiera pouted.

"Fine. I'll go get my car."

"Oh would you? I know it's not that far, but I'm exhausted."

Chen and Kiera went back inside the pub and ordered coffee whilst Cerys started the lonely trudge back to her cottage.

She wished she was able to transport herself like Kiera in that moment, but she couldn't. There were no portals in the village itself and she didn't want to draw attention by going into her closed shop, so she had no choice but to use her own feet to carry her.

Cerys removed her shoes as she reached her garden, and let the cool grass refresh her aching feet. She sighed with relief as she walked on.

Spying the puffs of steam rising up from her pond she approached and greeted Shui, Chen's dragon who'd taken up residence there.

"Hello, how are we today, Shw-aay?"

The little red dragon burbled quite contentedly as his body snaked through the water.

"At least someone's happy," she mused, leaving him to swim away.

He was really quite self-sufficient. He hunted his own food, and handily shrunk down to fit her small pond. It was hard to believe, looking at him like this, that she'd ridden on his back.

Cerys continued on to her vegetable patch, collected a trug basket from her small shed and dug up some fresh vegetables and then some herbs to take to Kiera. She whisked through her house, grabbing some milk and bread as well as some extra bottles of potions in case Pryderi needed them.

"No rest for the virtuous," she muttered out loud as she hurried to her car.

It was 'all go' recently. She had really hoped that Kiera and Pryderi would settle in the clan and she'd be able to have a brief respite. But no, fate wasn't that kind. She went out to her car, slung her goodies in the back and drove to collect Chen and Kiera from the pub.

Cerys bristled as she walked in to find Kiera's head resting on Chen's shoulder. But his look of 'I couldn't help it' assuaged her anger, and she realised Kiera had fallen asleep, despite the caffeine fix.

"OK, sleepyhead," she called, shaking her shoulders gently.

Kiera opened her bleary eyes a little, and softly groaned as Chen stood, taking her with him. His strong arm was supporting her as they crept out of the pub.

Fortunately, not many in the pub noticed, and those who did just disapprovingly dismissed the girl as being drunk.

"Shameful this time on a Sunday," Cerys heard someone mutter.

She didn't correct them. They managed to load the semi-conscious girl into the car, and deposited her onto the couch in Kiera's cottage.

"I don't like it. This is not normal," Cerys commented to Chen.

"Oh dear. What happened?" Frydah asked as she fluttered into view.

Her wings were working a little too quickly, thanks to her over indulgence of sugar.

"I don't know actually. But I'm starting to get worried."

"That makes two of us, if I'm honest. My senses are tingly, and not in a good way."

"Argh, this would be so much easier if I just had time to think. But I'm being pulled in two directions at once. Speaking of which, I need to go and check on Pryderi. Are you OK manning the fort here?" Cerys asked, swiping an ointment on Kiera's forehead.

"Of course," Frydah replied, her wings fluttering wildly still.

"Ha, maybe you can share some of that excess energy," Cerys smirked.

"May I come with you?" Chen enquired.

"Yes, please do. You can make sure I don't knock Rhion's stupid head off of his shoulders."

Chapter 5 – Pryderi's Progress

The pair of witches drove back to Cerys' house so they could use the portal in her garden to travel to the elinefae. Frydah had offered to zap them there, but Cerys declined. The faery's method of travel made her feel woozy, so she vowed to only use it in case of emergency.

They paused briefly before Cerys opened the gateway. It was just nice to be alone together for a moment.

"I'm so glad you're here," she whispered after sharing a brief kiss, her hands gently smoothing the back of Chen's head.

"I am glad to be here," he replied, bringing their foreheads together.

Feeling strengthened by her partner's presence, Cerys opened the portal at both ends.

She had not been able to do this until recently, and it was still a novelty. Previously, there had to be a witch at each end to open their respective portal openings. Lily had supposedly started this all off.

"I really should have been back sooner," she confessed as they stepped through.

"Kiera needed your help, she did not feel right accepting assistance from me yet. And you cannot be everywhere at once."

"I know. Just prepare yourself. She broke their cord, and he came off the worst of it."

They walked towards the encampment as they chatted, but halted their conversation as they approached elinefae ears. These people had highly sensitive hearing, and she didn't want to discuss too many details out in the open.

The pair headed straight for Pryderi's den, where Cerys suspected he still was. She wasn't wrong. He was still lying on his cot, but was conscious and in a lot less pain.

Cerys knelt on the floor as she looked into Pryderi's eyes, checking their clarity.

"How are you feeling?" she asked as she started her examination.

"*I do not know what is worse. The pain in my body or the pain of losing Kiera,*" he said, grimacing.

"That good, eh?" she smirked.

"May I?" Chen asked, kneeling next to Cerys.

Receiving her nod of agreement, he hovered his hand over Pryderi's bare abdomen. The boy was lying naked on the bed, but nobody was shy about it. Elinefae were very open about their bodies.

Chen channelled healing energy into the spot where Kiera had unwittingly cut their cord. He felt sorry for the poor girl. She must have truly believed Pryderi didn't love her to make this sort of separation. She literally tore herself away from him, at least in the etheric sense.

Focussing on seeing Pryderi's aura, Chen could see the wound which appeared as a gap in his light. Cerys' treatment had helped ease the pain, and even started the healing process. But worryingly, his emotional body had not yet healed. There was a black sort of goo which Chen pulled out on a spiritual level.

Chen's nose wrinkled as he also smelled a sort of charred sulphuric smell as he ensured all signs of the spectral goo were removed.

More elixir was applied to Pryderi's physical body by Cerys as Chen finished adding gentle energy to finally fix the emotional wound. A deep sigh escaped Pryderi's lips.

The physical pain he'd been feeling had now disappeared. And all he was left with was the gaping chasm in his heart and arms, the place where Kiera should be.

Pryderi slowly sat up, and dropped his legs to the floor, planting his elbows on his knees, with his hands supporting his downturned head.

"She's really gone," he muttered.

Chen rubbed the elinefae's upper arm soothingly.

Cerys was less sympathetic and told firmly him, "You made your choice."

Pained blue eyes glanced at her. "You should have let me die."

"No. Don't say that," Chen reprimanded.

"I cannot live without her, but I cannot live with her."

"Only for now. We will find a way. Trust me."

Electric blue eyes met chestnut brown as the two males committed to the silent promise. Pryderi felt Chen's support and was grateful for it. But he just couldn't see a way out of this mess. His head was filled with loneliness and despair.

"Come. It is near lunchtime. Let us get you some food," Chen said, offering his arm for Pryderi to help himself up with.

"I feel dizzy," Pryderi noted as he stood.

Chen exchanged a worried glance with Cerys. Elinefae had a supreme sense of balance, and should not ever feel dizzy.

Saying nothing, Chen helped Pryderi walk to the eating area. The amount of fresh air and exercise along with some food should help improve his health.

Chen plonked Pryderi onto a bench, and left Cerys to ensure he remained upright. He plated up some food from the offerings on the side.

Elinefae ate simple food, mainly living off what they and the forest grew. They didn't need to ingest blood every day, and eating cooked meat periodically helped sustain them. This clan had also discovered the benefits of coffee, which also lengthened the time between blood feedings.

There were some cold cuts of meat, which Chen heaped into a sandwich. He also grabbed some nuts and seeds, and poured some coffee.

Pryderi eagerly took his first bite into the sandwich, devouring it. But he immediately started to feel sick. He staggered to the bushes outside and promptly threw up.

Chen rushed to his side to offer aid. This really wasn't a good sign.

Cerys dashed to the cooks and requested some fresh blood. They always had some on standby in case of emergencies, and this definitely warranted it.

She took the cup over to the boys, who were still outside, but Pryderi was sitting on the ground. A crowd had started to gather, which Cerys shooed away. Pryderi gulped down the red liquid, despite Cerys trying to warn him to sip.

With a snarl, Pryderi leapt away. Cerys and Chen were left hoping he was hunting for food. There wasn't much they could do but wait.

On all fours, Pryderi bounded through the forest, in search of prey. He jumped up onto a tree trunk and pounced on a squirrel which had lingered for a second too long. He shook the body between his teeth, looking completely feral.

He sucked the body dry and let it fall limply onto the forest floor. It strengthened him, but didn't satisfy his hunger, which still gnawed at his stomach. Without thought for anything but his next victim, he sprinted over the roots at his feet.

There was a tapping sound. A rabbit was nearby and sending out a warning, stamping its foot. Pryderi honed in on the source. The rabbit had no chance. Pryderi's jaws were around its neck before it could even think of escape. His speed was no match for the poor creature.

Pryderi felt his life force fill with his prey's departed one. It flooded his system, rejuvenating every cell in his body. He tilted his head back and roared his satisfaction. He felt alive. He felt like himself again.

Shaking himself free from the invisible chains he now realised had been binding him, he made his way back to Cerys and Chen. He told them of the two curious feelings, of the invisible chains and his return to self.

"Well I'm glad you're feeling better. Take it easy today, and return to duty tomorrow. You know where I am if you need me," Cerys said, surprisingly calmly.

In their time alone, Chen had told her of the dark energy he'd removed. Matched with what Pryderi had just told her, she was getting a clearer idea of what was going on. And it wasn't good.

Chapter 6 – Healing

Cerys wanted to go and check on Kiera. Armed with the latest information, she was concerned for her wellbeing.

Kiera's mate's system had been completely shut down by the paranormal attack on him, but he at least seemed free of it now. But if he was free, was Kiera in greater danger now?

The pair hastened to Cerys' cottage, and went straight to Cerys' car through the garden once they were clear of the portal. Cerys was in a hurry.

They were met by nobody. Kiera's cottage was completely vacant. Panic clutched at Cerys' heart as she flew from room to room, calling to Kiera and Frydah, but receiving no response.

"I knew we shouldn't have left them," she shouted at Chen.

He calmly walked over to the coffee table and held up the note which was lying there, and waved it in front of Cerys' face.

Golden writing glowed into existence as she gazed at the formerly blank page.

'Dear Cerys,

We have gone to your house. Kiera insisted. She feels safer there apparently.

See you there.

Love Frydah'

"Oh right you are then," Cerys muttered.

Chen held out his arm as he offered, "Shall we?"

"I can't believe we drove all the way here when they were already back at mine," Cerys grumbled as she drove.

Chen sensibly remained silent as Cerys ranted all the way.

The girls were out in the garden when they got back. Kiera was stroking Shui, who was out of his pond for once, and had grown to cat size so she could better administer the attention he was happily receiving.

Sensing his companion's presence, the dragon padded over to Chen and nuzzled into his legs, winding himself between them.

"Why don't you two go put the kettle on?" Cerys said to Chen and Frydah.

She wanted to be alone with Kiera and check subtly for any signs of possession.

A small puff of smoke rose up as Shui snorted his displeasure at getting his hugs interrupted. He skulked back to the pond, shrank back to fit and slinked back into the water.

Cerys was actually a little encouraged. Dragons are extremely sensitive to dark energy, and whatever was lurking would've been picked up by Shui. She hoped.

The two girls strolled deeper into the garden together. Cerys sensed nothing attached to her, not even the wisp of a black tendril was hooked on. But she checked thoroughly, just to be sure.

Kiera breathed in deeply through her nose.

"Oh, that smell," she smiled.

"Which?"

Kiera approached the plant where it was coming from.

"This. It smells like me."

"Oh that," Cerys said, breathing a sigh of relief, "Yes, that's my azalea."

"Azaleas," she murmured, "Now I have my full elinefae name. Wait."

"What dear?"

"Oh my goddess. Cerys, that's why it was painful for him to be near me. Maybe subconsciously, but it hurt him."

"You're babbling, dear. Of whom are we talking?"

"My father. The girlfriend he lost, the witch he loved was named Azalea. He used to visit her. She would have grown them, right?"

"Well, quite probably."

"And he would have been able to detect my signature, wouldn't he?"

"Well, to some extent he would have known. He may not have been seeking it, due to his dislike of elinefae, but he may have sensed it anyway, I suppose."

"I smell of his dead girlfriend."

"Oh dear, do you have to phrase it quite like that?" Cerys asked with a shudder.

"Oh, you know what I mean. That's why he decided not to kill me. He couldn't. It would've been like killing her. Cerys, I know how to help him."

"Quite possibly, yes."

Kiera practically shouted through her mind link for Frydah to join her.

"Frydah, I know how to help him," she squealed as the faery popped into view.

"Pryderi? Oh goody. That was quick."

Kiera's excitement was suddenly diminished, her eyes lost their sparkle.

"No, not him, my father," she said meekly, looking at the ground.

"Oh. Sorry. Well that's still good."

"Come on, we have to go to his house."

Kiera vanished immediately, completely missing Cerys' words.

"Wait. I need to tell you something," she shrieked, but only Frydah heard.

"What? Quick? I need to go to her."

"There's some sort of dark force trying to leech onto her. I'm not quite sure what yet. But be careful."

"Dark entity. Got it," Frydah said as she disappeared from sight.

Kiera knew she was being impetuous. She was rushing to her father on a whim, without even having a clear plan. But she needed the distraction.

If she thought and moped about Pryderi for one more minute she feared for her sanity. Being apart from him was torture. It physically hurt and drained her.

Frydah fizzed into existence next to her, just outside the barrier Kiera had created. They went through it together.

Kiera's legs felt wobbly as she walked towards the house. She felt disoriented and confused. Her hand shot up to her forehead. She stopped walking as the world spun too fast, before collapsing in a heap. Frydah wasn't able to catch Kiera, but she did quickly grow the moss beneath her to cushion the fall.

Alerted by the disturbance of the threshold, Jeffers, the butler, was already on his way out to greet the guests. Upon seeing Threaris' daughter collapse he hurried to her aid.

"It's OK, Miss. I'm here," he comforted as he gently patted her cheeks.

Frydah was busy scanning for the dark energy Cerys had warned her of.

Hearing moaned signals she was coming to, Jeffers scooped Kiera up in his arms and carried her to the fortress of a house. He was surprisingly strong for a short old guy.

"Bring some water to her room," he commanded as he entered the foyer.

Frydah was a little surprised, but pleased to see a new servant. She felt sure this new addition at least had not been captured and forced into service as the previous ones had been.

Kiera had released all the people who her father had ensnared. Only the cook and the butler had remained. But it was a large residence, and required more staff to maintain it.

Kiera was laid softly down on the bed she'd used when she had been captured by her father. The suite of rooms was plush and airy. It was decorated in cream with soft gold highlights. It felt calming and tranquil here. Even in her imprisonment Kiera had felt like these rooms had been her refuge. It was only her father who had seemed imposing and frightening.

A jug of fresh water and glasses were swiftly brought in, and Jeffers helped Kiera sit up against her plump pillows, and sip the refreshing liquid.

"I'm sorry to be so much trouble, Jeffers," Kiera apologised groggily.

"Not at all, Miss."

"Kiera," she corrected.

"Of course, Miss," he replied, his smile creasing his eyes.

"What happened? I remember arriving…"

"You collapsed like a falling tree," Frydah informed her.

"Any idea why, oh helpful one?"

"Nope. Not a clue."

"Well, whatever the reason I think I actually feel better now."

"Really? That's weird," Frydah commented, scrunching her nose and peering at her friend curiously.

"And when was the last time I reacted normally to anything?" Kiera joked as she stood up.

"Well, there is that," she laughed back.

"I feel lighter."

"Well that's good," Frydah mused, hoping her friend had ditched whatever darkness had been lurking.

Kiera's stomach rumbled, making her confess, "And a little hungry."

"Say no more, Miss. I'll bring you both some refreshments in a jiffy. Please just rest and make sure you're recovered."

Kiera smiled at the butler's retreating back. He really was very sweet.

He soon returned with delicacies for both girls. As they munched, Kiera took the opportunity to quiz Jeffers on his knowledge of where Azalea had lived.

Feeling much better than she had in weeks, Kiera made her way to her father's room. She'd left him under a spell, forcing him to watch images of his past atrocities in the mirror in his room.

He was blocked from magick by the bracelet she'd crafted with the help of Frydah and her former maid now friend, Zondra. The aim was to show him the effects of what he'd done, the pain he'd caused in his quest to eliminate elinefae. In his attempt to stamp out his own grief, he'd inflicted far worse on others.

She stopped in her tracks, and her breath caught in her throat at the sight before her as she entered his room. Threaris was still sitting in his chair, sobbing uncontrollably. His eyes were red and swollen, his hair unkempt.

A male voice behind her spoke up, "He would have scratched himself to pieces without your careful words, Miss. But he can cause no harm, not even unto himself."

"He's so dishevelled. I hoped he'd be better than this by now."

"Regrettably, he seems to sink further into despair."

"His atrocities have been great."

"Indeed, a great many, Miss. And he now feels the horror of those acts."

"He must be sorry for them?"

"I think so, but he has still not said as much. When he speaks it is to plead for no more. He cannot bear to see it all."

"Still feeling sorrier for himself, by the sounds of it," she mused.

Her resolve strengthened as she listened to the butler. Yes, he needed to realise the full extent of what he'd done, but he also needed to repent.

"Get up. You are coming along with me," she commanded the wreck in the chair.

He stood on wobbling legs, and slumped his way towards her, not even looking in her direction. His eyes were vacant and glazed.

Having received details on the location from Jeffers, she took her father's hand and transported them to an abandoned elinefae encampment.

Chapter 7 – Remember Her

Nature had started reclaiming the remnants of elinefae life which had once dwelt here, and Kiera had to magickally hack away vines to get to the entrance of the warren of dens in the abandoned encampment.

Her father followed unwittingly. He was lost to the world and cared not where he was.

Frydah flitted behind, trying to ensure their safety. She constructed a temporary shield around their small party. This place was spooky.

Hoping this clan had followed the same layout, Kiera led Threaris down the dark tunnels. Chills ran through her despite the warmth. She felt as if they were intruding on a tomb, which she supposed they were to some extent.

Her father's presence did nothing to comfort her either. He was creepy before, but like this he was totally unnerving.

Even now, she could sense the magickal essence of a witch's presence. It was like a ghost leading the way to the door she was seeking.

Kiera yelped as the candles on the walls lit as she opened the door. Oh, she hoped this dwelling was not truly haunted. Even Frydah flitted backwards a little in alarm, and decided to stay on guard just outside the room.

Taking a steadying breath, Kiera led Threaris into what was once Azalea's room. There was a flicker of recognition in her father's eyes.

"I know this place," he murmured hoarsely, staring around him.

"Tell me about the woman who dwelled here," Kiera encouraged.

Threaris blinked a few times, his eyes starting to clear.

"Azalea. This was Azalea's den. Oooohhhh Azalea," he wailed, his knees falling onto the floor.

"Why did you bring me here?" he cried, "Have I not suffered enough?"

"You need to remember her, and honour her memory."

He pulled himself along the floor towards the bed. He clutched the blanket which still lay there, and held it to him, sniffing her lingering scent.

"Why can she not be here?" he wailed.

"People die, Threaris. You of all people should know this, having been responsible for extinguishing many lives yourself."

"But it wasn't her time."

"And all those lives you claimed. Was it their time?"

"Yes, they had been responsible for her death. They no longer deserved to live."

"You truly feel this?"

"Yes. No. I don't know. I just want her."

"You know you cannot. Not in this lifetime."

"Then let me die. I will go to her."

"No. You will be condemned."

"What have I done?" he bemoaned the phrase which had become his mantra.

Helping him sit on the bed, Kiera compelled, "You will remain here and think of Azi. You will contemplate the happy times. You may fall asleep should you need to."

Theraris let his torso flop onto the bed. He curled up into a ball and had no choice but to think of his life with Azalea.

It was a bittersweet torture. He remembered the smell of her own flowers, the herbal teas she'd make them, the touch of her skin, the taste of her lips on his. But all the time he still felt the emptiness of his loss.

Over one hundred and fifty years had done nothing to diminish his pain. More tears fell down his cheeks. He whimpered her name as memories flooded his mind. Eventually he fell asleep.

Kiera had been sitting on a stool in the far corner of the room, keeping an eye on him, making sure he was OK. It pained her to see her father go through this. She had to keep reminding herself it was for his own good.

Now he was asleep she crept closer to the bed, and magnified her signature scent. The smell of azaleas wafted over the bed.

"Mmmm, Azalea," Threaris murmured.

Kiera was careful to keep a safe distance away from him, even though he was sleeping.

"Yes, it is I," she whispered the lie, hating herself for what she was about to do.

"I miss you."

"You must let me go to my rest."

"But I need you, Azalea. Don't leave me."

"I left long ago. But you are tethering me here unfairly."

"I love you."

"I love you too," she whispered, and shockingly realised she actually meant those words.

"Please don't go," he said, starting to thrash around on the bed.

"I must. I will wait for you. We will meet again."

"Do you forgive me? Can you?"

"Forgive what?"

"I am sorry, Azalea. I am sorry for dishonouring you, for all I have done since you left me. I was crazed with despair. I thought I was avenging you. I was controlled by something greater than me."

"Death does not kill death."

"I know that now. I can never make it right. The things I've done."

He was curling up again, and groaning his remorse.

"You will stop."

"Yes Azalea. I'll stop. I vow to never kill another soul."

"Then I forgive you."

"You do? You truly forgive me?" as he shouted these words he sat up, wide awake and alert.

Kiera quickly zapped herself back to her stool. Threaris gazed around the room frantically.

"Where is she? Where did she go?" he asked, his eyes wild.

Showing a calm exterior, whilst inwardly trembling, she asked, "Who?"

"Azalea. She was here, Kiera, she was here. She forgives me."

Kiera smiled as best she could through her fear. "That is good."

"Oh, I was wrong, Kiera. So wrong. The dead *can* forgive."

He was up on his feet now, his hands held towards the heavens.

Keeping her distance, Kiera tried to calm him.

"So now you must seek more."

"More?"

"You must seek forgiveness for all the lives you stole."

"Yes. Oh yes. I will. How? Where? Tell me what I must do."

"Are you truly repentant?"

He sank down to the floor on one knee.

"How can you ask me this? Look at me. Yes, I truly repent," he said thrusting his hands out in supplication.

"Very well, take my hand," she instructed, stretching out her trembling fingers towards his.

"You are scared of me?"

"I am afraid for you."

"Please don't be. Not now. Kiera, I will be well."

"I hope so."

She nodded at Frydah in the doorway, who was free to transport herself.

The candles blew out and she could have sworn she heard a female voice say thank you. Shivers zapped through her as Kiera transported herself and her father to his home, to his library.

***

Threaris stared at the scroll above the fireplace, the one with his curse written upon it. He started to understand its true meaning now.

He turned to look at his daughter, but a golden light caught his attention.

"Oh Frydah, you are here," he said.

His vision and head felt clearer somehow, like a dark misty veil had been lifted.

"I apologise to you. I hurt you dreadfully. And you would be within your rights to harm me as just punishment."

A thought occurred to him, and he narrowed his eyes.

"But you did not harm me, did you? You had ample opportunity. No, you helped care for me."

"You can thank your daughter for that. I was acting under her instruction."

"Ah, I see. She compelled you. That explains it."

"No. She showed me another way. She made me let go of my anger. Pity replaced it as I saw what you were going through."

"Pity?"

"I think that is the correct word. You were hurting and I felt sad for you. You did not need me to harm you. You were doing that yourself."

He nodded his acknowledgement, and turned towards Kiera.

"Kiera, my daughter. I acted shamefully towards you. You grew up isolated from any real family. When you learned of your true father, and should have had his love and support, you received the very opposite. I am so sorry. Can you forgive a foolish old sorcerer?"

His look of regret was so sincere that if she hadn't done so already she would have forgiven him on the spot. She took his hands in hers.

"I forgive you," she whispered through her tears.

Her father for the first time in her life hugged her. He sobbed into her shoulder, and begged forgiveness over and over.

She rubbed his back and soothed, "It's OK. It's all going to be OK. We forgive you."

He leaned back slightly and looked into her eyes.

"Oh my beautiful daughter. Can you reply on behalf of all elinefae and all magickal beings? You represent all, do you not? If I beg their forgiveness through you, will it be granted?"

"Try it," she urged.

Kneeling on one knee he held out his arms dramatically and formally announced:

To all beings I have harmed,

I offer apology overdue.

My ire has now been disarmed,

I am truly sorry unto you.

"And you truly mean that, Threaris?" a sneering voice questioned, seemingly out of nowhere.

"Althea, you are here? Yes, yes, I am sorry."

The haughty sorceress bowed down and peered deep into his clear green eyes.

"Yes," she drooled out, "Yes, I believe you are. It took you long enough."

"Perhaps. But perhaps it would not have taken quite so long had someone cared to show me the way."

"Well, in that it seems this young girl has shown great wisdom." She nodded towards Kiera as she spoke.

"Yes, I am in her debt," he replied, hugging his daughter to him again, and kissing her hands.

"Then I fully release you into her capable care."

Althea turned her attention to Kiera.

"Once he is fully himself again you may wish to alter that clever little bracelet. Allow him magick with certain limitations perhaps?"

Without ceremony the sorceress disappeared from the room just as swiftly as she'd entered, leaving the others in stunned silence.

Chapter 8 – Happy Sad

Threaris was once more left alone with Kiera. He looked at her with new eyes. His curse had been lifted, and his mind had been opened to what had happened. No darkness remained.

He was dumbfounded. It was all so clear now. Had he really done all those things? He couldn't have. But all those images he'd been shown in the mirror; it must be true. The thought of all those atrocities almost brought him to his knees.

Kiera helped him to his feet, and guided him to a chair by the fire which she magickally lit. She also called Jeffers to request some tea.

Walking into the room, the trusty butler's jaw dropped.

"Master," he breathed as he bowed.

He approached and put a trembling hand on Threaris' shoulder.

"You're back. It's really you," he choked out around the lump in his throat.

Threaris rose to his feet and man hugged his butler. A most unseemly act, but allowable under the circumstances.

"Yes, I am truly home," Threaris reassured Jeffers, "Thanks to my daughter."

Said daughter was looking on, perplexed. These two males were acting as if Threaris hadn't been here. But this place is exactly where he'd been tethered for over a century.

"Oh my beautiful daughter," Threaris called, stretching his arms wide.

As soon as she entered his embrace she immediately began to understand what they were on about. He felt different.

"Father," she declared, tears trickling down her face again.

Her face nestled into his shoulder as she sobbed. She couldn't stop it. Relief washed over her. The man holding her so lovingly now was truly her father. The one she'd not even known existed.

Jeffers had discreetly exited the room to fetch some celebratory Champagne. The popping noise of the cork made them both jump. They parted to look over at the butler.

"Apologies, Sir," Jeffers said with a smirk.

"Ooh bubbles," Frydah squealed as she flitted over.

Jeffers carefully poured some Champagne into a faery sized glass for her, which made her grin with delight.

"Oh, how considerate. Thank you," she said as she took the glass.

"To being yourself," Threaris toasted once they all had a glass, even Jeffers.

They all chinked glasses and sipped. Frydah giggled as she the bubbles tickled her nose. Emptying his glass, Threaris excused himself with a shallow bow.

"I am incredibly tired after these exertions. Please excuse me."

Jeffers scurried out with his master, ensuring he reached his room safely.

Kiera turned her frowning face to the faery, but Frydah reassured her. "It's to be expected. He's finally free from whatever spell, or I think spells he's been under. It must have taken an awful lot out of him."

"Spells plural?"

"Yes. Seeing him now, he's totally different. Hmm, he seems quite nice actually. Who would've thought it?"

"Frydah. Be nice."

"Sorry, but it's all a bit of a surprise. Anyway, I'm sure he'll feel better after a nap. So, what shall we do now?" she asked fluttering wildly.

"Well first I need to contact Cerys," Kiera said.

"Oh poo. Boring."

"Come on," she replied, rolling her eyes and starting to walk away.

***

Kiera used the dressing table mirror in her room to call her friend.

"Oh there you are, dear. Is everything OK?"

"Better than OK. Cerys, it worked. My dad, he's better."

"That's good, dear."

"No. Like better better. He's him. I can see him. Who he really is."

Cerys scowled.

"Multiple spells removed," Frydah added, flitting into view.

"Multiple? Oh dear. So there was dark magick involved?"

"Uh huh, looks like it," the faery slurred.

"Have you been drinking?" Cerys asked, raising an eyebrow.

"Jeffers wanted to celebrate the sorcerer's return. The sorcerer is psycho no more."

"And where is he now?"

"He got sleepy. He's taking a nap," Frydah said in a babyish voice.

"Well, I suppose that's OK. Kiera, are you coming back home?"

"Um, I was sort of thinking I might stay here a bit. I want to make sure he's OK anyway. But…"

"Of course you want to get to know your father. Perfectly understandable. Especially now he's truly himself."

"You don't mind?"

"Why would I mind? I'll smooth things over with Annie tomorrow."

"Oh, the coffee shop," Kiera gasped.

"Will be just fine. It's the least of your problems at the moment."

"Maybe, but I still don't like letting people down."

"Ever good." Frydah grinned. "Unlike that Althea. Eurgh, she's so snooty."

"Oh, don't mention her," Cerys moaned, grimacing.

"She came to fully release his curse."

"Could that have been the other spell you sensed?"

"That would be nice, but no. There was definitely something dark too, but it's gone now. You were right."

"Right? Dark? Am I missing something?" Kiera interjected.

"I'll explain later," Frydah hushed her.

"I'd better go anyway, people to see, things to do," Cerys chimed, waving goodbye before her image disappeared.

"She never stops being odd." Kiera sighed, slumping back into her chair.

"You look like you could do with a nap too."

"Yeah, maybe," she admitted, slowly making her way to her big feathery bed.

But as she flolloped onto the comfy mattress, images of her and Pryderi filled her head, and they completely dulled her sparkle.

She thought of how she'd transported him here without realising what she was doing. She'd been separated from him then too. The pain had been just as great, but her blood lust had added to it.

She had brought him right here into her room where they'd made wild passionate love together. A deep sigh escaped her lips. She missed Pryderi so much. Her father's plight had indeed been a distraction, but now her own pain hit with full force, squeezing the air out of her lungs.

She missed his electric blue eyes, and the way they glowed orange in the dark. She missed running her fingers through his long black hair and down his chiselled cheeks. And those oh so plump lips that kissed her so wonderfully.

Kiera breathed in deeply, remembering his enchanting forest fragrance. Before she knew it the elinefae in her mind stood before her in her room.

"Oops."

"Kiera," he gasped as he ran to pick her up in his strong arms.

They covered each other in kisses. A small golden glow broke in between the pair and slapped them both on the nose.

"What do you think you're doing?"

"I didn't mean to." Kiera pouted, fighting to get back to her mate.

"He's supposed to be with his clan."

"No. He's supposed to be with me, but some idiot has decided otherwise."

"I can't argue with that." Frydah shrugged. "But if that idiot Leader finds out, you'll both be in serious trouble."

"I was on duty. Alone." Pryderi smirked. "Nobody will notice."

Frydah audibly gasped. "And you would neglect your duty?"

"To be with Kiera? Yes," he said, finally managing to brush past the faery's barrier.

He picked up where he'd left off, planting kisses over his mate's face and neck, pulling her close to his body. He needed her like an addict needs a fix, and Kiera was his drug.

"By the goddess, I missed you," he whispered between kisses.

"Argh, I give up," Frydah huffed as she vanished away from the illicit pair.

They didn't notice. They were too busy devouring each other, tearing at their clothing to get contact skin-to-skin.

Kiera fell back on the bed, her legs beckoning him to where they both needed him to be.

With a deep rumbling growl, he dived on top of her, and plunged straight in, making her come instantly. The sweet blessed release coursed through her body like a lightning bolt.

Her fingernails clawed into his shoulders, seeking more of him. Her hips thrust to meet his.

They were both gasping, panting with their deep lust that demanded satisfaction.

Being pulled apart had been utter torture. This was pure bliss.

Pryderi cried out as he surged forwards, revelling in the sensation of his beloved Kiera's muscles gripping onto his cock.

Their bodies intertwined and meshed, echoing the merging of their souls. It was as if they'd been drowning and were now surfacing for air.

Shivers ran down her spine as Pryderi licked her neck.

She pulled her knees up and clenched onto his buttocks, drawing him in ever further.

"Oh Kiera," he hissed as he climaxed, bringing her over the edge with him.

Pryderi brushed cheek to cheek before nuzzling into her neck.

"I missed you so much," he whispered.

"I missed you too," she sighed.

His lips brushed hers in a tender kiss before he shuffled around so he could spoon her. His muscular arm wrapped possessively around her waist. Her bum wriggled into his groin.

"You chose them though," she simpered sadly.

"Not like that. No. Before you, I made a blood oath to clan. There was no choice. Could you think otherwise?"

"I did. In that moment I thought so."

"Oh my love." He sighed, nuzzling into her neck. "Always you."

"I'm sorry."

"For what?"

"For doubting you."

"I understand. You did not know. Rhion was wrong. He should not have treated you that way. And he should not have offered a choice which could not be made."

"Cerys explained."

"It is not like him. Something is wrong."

"We know. We're still trying to work it out. But we will."

"I know you will."

Kiera wiggled around in his arms so she could look into his bright blue eyes.

"You know?"

"You are clever. I trust you," he told her with a kiss.

"Wow, you really do believe in me."

"Of course. You are my mate," he smiled, his eyes shining with love.

"But for now I must send you back before you're missed," she admitted.

The words sounded worse out loud than they had in her head. They needed to separate again, and it tore her heart out to do it.

"Wait. Why are you here? Your father has not..?"

"No, no. Oh, I cured him. He's completely better now. I think he will need to make peace with what's happened. But he is no longer under any spells."

"See. Clever," he said with another kiss.

Her hand cupped the back of his head so she could deepen that kiss.

She struggled to pull her lips away, and replaced them with her forehead. "How am I going to do this?"

"Not forever."

"No. We will find a way to be together, won't we?"

"Of course."

She started to summon the magickal energy.

"Um, perhaps I should clothe?" he suggested with a cheeky smile.

"Oh right," she agreed, blushing.

She was very attentive as he slunk off the bed and put his clothes on. She didn't want to say goodbye to those muscly thighs, or that fine…washboard stomach, she thought as she glanced over his magnificent manhood. She cursed his trousers as they slid up and over, hiding it from view.

He shrugged his waistcoat style leather top on over his well-defined chest.

Kiera cast a quick protection spell over him, just in case anything went wrong when he got back to his home.

"Come here," he called, beckoning her to him.

He gathered her into his arms once more. He held onto her, trying to cling on to every detail so he could remember this moment forever.

"I love you," he uttered on a whisper.

"I love you too," she whimpered.

Snatching one last lingering kiss she finally shook herself free, trying to steady her senses which had been shaken by his presence.

"Ready?" she asked.

With sorrow dulling his eyes, he slowly nodded.

With grim determination, she reluctantly concentrated on where he had been and sent him back there.

'Back to the idiot Leader,' she thought with a lip curl.

Chapter 9 – In the Dark

It was stifling in her room, Kiera needed some fresh air. Of course, it had nothing to do with having to say goodbye to Pryderi again. Not at all. But how many times would they have to part? She stomped through the hall and out through the front door, blind to everything except her frustration.

'Yes, that's right. Come out here,' a sinister voice sounded in her head.

Kiera's feet carried on walking towards her barrier. Nobody could cross it if they intended to harm her father. He had no way of properly defending himself since she'd banned him from using magick.

"Kiera, where are you going?" someone was calling from the house.

But she walked on regardless, deaf to all. She wanted to cross, to walk far away from here.

'You want to go to the beach.'

Yes, that's where she wanted to go. She wanted to walk down the cliff path and go to the sea.

Kiera finally felt the tiny hand banging on her forehead.

"Hey dummy head, stop. Where are you going?" the furious faery was ranting at her.

"Um, to the beach, I think," she replied, scratching her head.

"Oh no you don't. You march straight back into that house, young lady," Frydah commanded, sending golden sparks flying.

It took all of Frydah's powers of compulsion, but Kiera finally obeyed. Jeffers and Threaris had hurried into the entrance hall, alerted by the commotion.

"What's going on?" Threaris asked.

"Someone decided to randomly go for a walk," Frydah muttered.

"She is not allowed to go for a walk?"

"Oh, did I forget to mention it was at the command of a creepy voice?"

"Kiera, look at me," Threaris said, drawing her face in his direction with his fingers.

"Freddy," Frydah screeched her faery helper's name.

A dark orange glow appeared.

"You called?" he asked cheerfully.

"Yes. Go see where that creepy voice came from," she instructed.

The dark brown faery disappeared from view.

Threaris was looking at Kiera's eyes which still looked hazy. Grabbing his daughter's hand, he practically dragged her down the hall. He led her down a spiral staircase, which was hidden from view by a concealed door.

Kiera had never been down here, but didn't have the energy to give it much consideration. Threaris opened a door to the sort of laboratory you see in films about wizards or old fashioned scientists.

There were wooden benches, and all sorts of glass bottles adorned shelves along the walls. Jeffers had accompanied them, and lit a Bunsen burner without having to be asked.

Threaris grabbed bottles of blue and yellow liquids and poured them into a cylinder. Using tongs, Jeffers held the cylinder in the flame and swirled until it bubbled and formed a vivid green colour.

Taking hold of the tongs, Threaris wafted the bottle under Kiera's nose.

"Inhale," he told her.

"Sniff that?" she asked, pulling a 'not on your life' face.

"Just do it please," he said, rolling his eyes.

"You're sure he's good now?" Frydah asked mischievously at Kiera's ear.

"I hope so," she said, taking in a deep breath of green mist, which now had an ominous glow.

"Eurgh, that smells like sewage," she declared with a wince.

Her eyes fully cleared and were back to their usual vivid green. She shook her head as if that too still needed clearing.

"What was that?" she asked.

"Some sort of dark energy. My first guess would be a daoi-sith, but I reserve judgement," her father pronounced as calmly as if he were stating the weather was fine today.

"A daoi-sith? What makes you say that? Nobody even saw it," Frydah challenged.

"The border is overhung by the upper cliff face, there's plenty of shadows for it to hide in. The disembodied voice. The very fact none of us saw it. The efficacy of the clearing potion, and the fact that the potion glowed. But I can't be sure."

"What's a *dowy-sith*?" Kiera asked.

"Nasty chaps with glowing eyes and pointy ears. Known as dark elves to some. Dark as in the places where they dwell, only in the shadows, not unlike elinefae, but malevolent. They are also pale in appearance," her father informed her.

"But not elinefae?" Kiera checked, alarmed at how similar they sounded to her own kind.

"No. Not related at all oddly, despite appearances."

"But they could be mistaken for them if you saw one?"

A terrible thought crossed her father's mind.

"I suppose so, yes," he muttered.

Satisfied his daughter's aura was cleared of any dark forces thanks to his potion, he hurried them all out of his lab, muttering as he did so.

"I must do some research, some investigating," he wittered.

Threaris hastened to his library where he could supposedly bury himself in books. Whilst Jeffers led the faery and Kiera back to her suite.

"All clear," Freddy announced, re-joining them.

"Please do not go back outside yet, Miss. You should be safe here, I think," the butler advised, backing towards the door.

"Wait. Please. My father is disturbed. What is the matter?"

"Daoi-sith are incredibly devious and can hide in the shadows, unseen."

"You think it's possible one of these caused my father's illness, don't you?"

"Miss, it is entirely possible it *was* your father's illness."

"But surely he would have known?"

"Not if it took hold before he was aware of its presence, Miss."

"But you would have noticed something."

"I am afraid Miss, that it now seems possible that although I knew something was amiss, that perhaps I did not realise the full extent of the problem myself."

"He cleared me just now though, with that potion. All those years, did neither of you try?"

"Of course we did." The butler bristled at the accusation of negligence.

He brushed off his sleeves before continuing, "The potion you just received would not clear a possession. It merely cleared anything that had touched your aura remotely. We tried so many things."

A rueful look of sadness crossed Jeffers' face as he stated this last fact.

"Of course you did. I'm sorry, I didn't mean to imply any wrong doing. I was just surprised and curious."

"I believe Althea's curse may have only added to the complication, but we will need to look into the matter. Please Miss, I beg leave to return to my master to assist."

"Oh yes, of course. Please go. But please let me know if I can help."

Jeffers bowed smartly and vacated the room.

"I think you upset him," Freddy commented, not terribly helpfully.

"Oh hello, we've not properly met. I'm Kiera," she said towards the golden brown glow which kept darting around her head.

"Yes, I know. I'm Freddy. Pleased to meet you," he said, slowing down enough so she could see him properly.

She noticed his skin was a darker golden brown than Frydah's. His eyes were brown, flecked with bright orange. And his hair was dark brown and messy, more like a bird's nest than hair.

"So, what do you two know of daoi-sith?" Kiera asked with a sigh.

Chapter 10 – Faith

Pryderi was completely unaware of the peril his mate was in. He was back on his well-worn route. Happily, he had been correct in his assumption that nobody would miss him when he was with Kiera.

He had been clinging onto the blissful memories as he wandered along his path. On one hand he was incredibly grateful for the brief reunion. It was a terrific experience, and the relief of seeing his mate again was indescribably wonderful.

But now he was left alone, cold and empty again. He longed to hold Kiera in his arms, to feel her comforting presence, and show her his home. He had planned their life so differently.

He thought of how they had met. Having caught the briefest glimpse of her when she wandered into his territory whilst jogging, his interest had been piqued. He'd had no idea of who or what she was.

She hadn't even smelled like a true elinefae then. She'd not transitioned, and the smell of the humans she lived amongst pervaded her clothing. But still he'd been interested. Something had instantly told him he had to be with her, no matter what.

He had been the one destined to collect the clan's coffee order from the shop where she worked the night which had sealed their fate.

They had kissed, against the laws of his clan. He had still thought she was at least part human, which meant she was strictly off limits. But he'd not been able to help himself. And then she'd kissed him back.

That's when it happened. Their kiss had triggered off her transition. Her elinefae DNA won out as her body painfully reformed.

He had thought of them as inseparable from that moment, and even more so once they'd made love for the first time. But her father had come along and kidnapped her.

That hadn't been able to stop them though. She'd unwittingly transported her to him. Her sorceress skills had also been heightened by her transition.

Pryderi harrumphed as he thought, 'Well, if a sorcerer couldn't keep us apart I don't see why a Leader should be able to.'

They had been united heart, body and soul. That phrase is perhaps overused, but not in their case. They were a soul matched mated pair. Nothing should be able to keep them apart.

Pryderi was so proud of her. She had been through so much in such a short space of time. More than any elinefae ever should have to go through. And yet she was strong.

If he was completely honest, her sorceress power was sexy. He loved the raw power that flowed around and through her. And the things she could do were simply amazing.

Pryderi had some limited magick, being elinefae. But hers was marvellous, and he thought there may be more she was yet to learn. He smiled as he thought how extraordinary Kiera was.

After their meeting, he had begun to feel better about their situation. Now he had time to reflect he realised this was only temporary. He trusted in his mate, believed in her power and had faith she would find a way of being with him. And their link was a reassuring presence again.

Pryderi paused as he approached the sacred area. This is where she'd first bumped into him, literally. He chuckled at the memory of their clumsiness. It was most unlike him, but not totally unlike her, he'd discovered.

He let his senses reach out, ensuring he was alone. He reverently stepped into the sacred circle, and knelt down by the central stone. Biting into his hand he let a few drops trickle onto the hallowed rock.

"*I swear my mate and I will be together, come what may, I pledge myself unto her,*" he solemnly declared to the goddess they worshipped here.

As if in answer to his oath, the sun chose that moment to emerge from behind a cloud and shone down on Pryderi. He basked in the glory of its warm light.

Licking his bite marks to heal himself, he held his hand to his heart.

"*Thank you goddess. Harm none. So mote it be,*" he uttered in hushed tones as he dipped his head in deference.

Pryderi bit his lip as he stood and slowly backed away. He shook his head and chuckled at himself.

"*I am getting as bad as my mate,*" he mused, having caught himself mimicking Kiera's lip biting habit.

'That is two blood oaths I have now sworn. I wonder which is stronger?' he thought, surprised at his own actions.

It had been a spur of the moment thing, a mere whim. But he had meant it. He knew if it truly came down to it, he would put Kiera's life before clan. That was what a soul-matched mate did. But now he'd vowed as much.

The rest of his shift passed by peacefully. He strolled around the boundary at leisure, enjoying the warmth of the rare sunshine.

He was unusual in his fondness for the shining orb. Most of his kind lived in the darkness and preferred it. But not Pryderi. He was glad to take the day shifts.

As the sun went down, he finally wandered into the dining area to get his dinner as most of the clan helped themselves to their breakfast.

Pryderi sat on his own at the end of a long bench, zoning out the noisy hubbub of the early risers. He was not alone long however. He noticed Elan's shoulders rolling as he walked to join him. He had a confident swagger, and was much sought after.

Elinefae are highly sexualised and not fussy over which sex satisfies their urges. And Elan had satisfied a great many. He was still unmated and planned on staying that way.

There was a time when Pryderi had felt the same. But not now. He'd not so much as looked at another clan member in a sexual manner since he'd bonded with his mate.

His friend's heavy hand clapped Pryderi on the shoulder as he joined him on the bench.

"*How goes it, brother?*" Elan asked in his usual jovial manner, his violet eyes glimmering with mirth.

"*I fare well.*"

"*Yes, I see this. You are brighter than you have been of late. It is good to see.*"

"*I have found hope, my friend.*"

"*Ooh, intriguing.*"

"*Not much to tell. I have but decided to trust in my mate.*"

"*Eurgh, mate. A tragedy. But so be it. If you are meant to be you will be.*" Elan had a flare for the dramatic, and gestured wildly as he spoke, striking his forehead with the back of his hand.

"*Fate brought us together, and I trust it will bring us together again.*"

"*A much healthier way to view things, my friend. Ah, Arwyn, our brother here has hope,*" he taunted, beckoning their friend over.

"*I am pleased to hear this,*" Arwyn smiled as he ruffled Pryderi's hair.

Pryderi shrugged off his friend's irritating hand. Arwyn's response was to nudge him with his hip so he could sit on the end of the bench with his own dinner. He had also just come off shift.

They chatted nonchalantly whilst they ate. Pryderi's mood was buoyed by the interaction. It was just like old times, and it made him happier. He felt lucky to have such good friends around him.

Arwyn and Pryderi bade farewell to Elan who was just going onto shift, a little late, but others were already about.

"*Do you go straight to bed, brother?*" Arwyn asked Pryderi once they were alone, and had strolled away from the dining area.

"*I had been, but do you have something else in mind?*"

"*I wanted to seek private conversation with you. But if you are tired I do not wish to detain you.*"

"*I do not think I will find sleep easily. You sound serious. Are you alright?*" he asked, his brows furrowing as he looked at his friend from the corner of his eye.

"*Me? I am fine, my friend. I wanted to ask if you are really as cheery as you appear,*" Arwyn said as they carried on walking away from the rest of the clan.

"*Yes. I thank you. I am fine.*"

"*Forgive me, but it is a remarkable transformation. May I ask what has brought this about?*"

"*Do you ask for yourself or for Rhion?*"

"*Me, of course,*" Arwyn replied, his lip curling at the insinuation.

"*My apologies. So much has been unusual of late. I needed to check. Please forgive me.*"

"*Always. And I even understand. The wrongness is why I wanted to check with you. The atmosphere feels strange. And Rhion's decision was so out of character. It is confusing.*"

"*I agree. I have tried to be extra vigilant on watch, but I have found nothing.*"

"*Me neither. But tell me, have you a plan? Is this why you are happier?*"

"*No. No plan, my friend. I just have faith.*"

"*Faith? You have prayed to the goddess and now you are happy?*" he mocked.

"*No. I have faith in Kiera.*"

"*Ah, to believe in one's mate is good. To have faith in one's mate when she is a sorceress is wise. If anyone can help she can.*" Arwyn smiled, putting his arm around Pryderi's shoulder.

"If I ask it, would you help us?"

"Help, even against clan's ruling?"

"Yes. Would you?" Pryderi's own electric blue eyes were earnestly locked onto Arwyn's pale blue ones as he asked the unaskable.

"For you, my brother, yes. I have pledged my oath to protect clan. You are in the right. To come to your aid is to uphold that oath, not a betrayal of it."

The two males hugged it out before finally parting ways to find whatever rest would be granted to their troubled minds.

Chapter 11 – Guided to the Light

Kiera used her dressing table mirror to contact Cerys. Having exchanged pleasantries, Kiera brought up the uncomfortable subject.

"My father thinks there is a daoi-sith about. It may be what tried to attack me here. I'm fine, Threaris managed to rescue me. Frydah thinks my shield is keeping its physical presence at bay."

"Oh my, a dark elf? I've not heard of them for many a year. I thought the light elves and elinefae had wiped them all out. Well, that would explain the dark energy I thought I felt. Oh dear. What are we to do?"

"Threaris is looking into it. But he thinks I should stay here until the threat is eliminated."

"Yes, that seems wise. I'll speak with Annie. She must be getting fed up of your prolonged illness by now."

"Oh no, poor Annie. I'd not thought of that. So much for me returning to a normal life."

Frydah's glow flittered into view in the mirror.

"If I may suggest, Freddy and I thought the fae realm may be more suitable. If what Threaris says is correct, this daoi-sith may be what held him under attack all these years. With Kiera's power and connection with the sorcerer, it may be better to completely remove her from harm's way."

"Well, she may be safer with the fae, but it seems rather extreme. And I must say I'm not entirely sure safe is the best word. No offense Frydah, but some of the fae can be rather tricky."

"But I'd be there with her," the faery huffed.

"Can we call it plan B? Maybe once we're sure it really is a daoi-sith, and if the threat seems to increase then would be the time to take her?"

"Fine, but if he gets her it's not my fault."

"Agreed. This is my decision," Cerys said, her hackles rising.

"Oh, and you should probably increase the shield at your place and over the clan."

Chen's face peered at the side of the mirror, partially obscuring Cerys.

"I can help with that," he smiled.

Chen had dealt with many dark entities in his homeland. One daoi-sith shouldn't be too hard to defeat. He dashed outside straight away, grabbing some black salt and clary sage oil from his girlfriend's supply cupboard en route.

By the time he came back inside, having scattered the protection ingredients around the property, and ensuring all negative energy was banished, Cerys had finished her call with Kiera.

He saw her worried face and strode over to the witch.

He brushed his thumb along her cheek as he soothed, "It's OK. We can fight this."

"I hope you're right," Cerys replied, still frowning.

Chen held her closely and rubbed her shoulders, making her sigh.

Cerys could have a gruff and wise exterior, but it masked a squishy underbelly. She cared deeply for those within her care, and had worked tirelessly over the years to create and maintain peace for her clan. And now that precious peace was under threat.

"I will travel to the clan tomorrow, and strengthen their defences," he assured her.

"That leaves me with the shop and finding a suitable excuse for Kiera's boss."

"It would seem I have the better job," he chuckled.

Of course, that chuckle earned him a friendly slap on the arm. But that was quickly followed by a loving kiss.

***

Mid-morning the following day, Cerys snuck out of her store and along to the coffee shop where Kiera should have been working.

The bell chimed as she hurried in through the door, and approached the counter, all ready with a brilliant excuse. But then she saw Annie.

The witch's jaw dropped open. She was just about to say something until she saw the barely perceptible shake of the coffee shop owner's head. It was then that Cerys realised there was a customer in the shop, sitting at a table, calmly drinking coffee.

"Oh hello, Janet," Cerys flustered, trying to appear calm.

"Hello, long time no see," the hair salon owner greeted.

"I know, I am overdue an appointment," Cerys admitted, her hand fluffing her hair.

Cerys' accent always had a Welsh twang, but it was heightened by stress or the same accent in others she spoke with. Both were present right then.

"Pop by later and book yourself in," Janet encouraged, apparently completely oblivious whose presence she was in.

"I'll do that. But how do you come to be here at this time?" Cerys was doing her best to sound normal and breezy, but her curiosity and awe were putting up a fight.

"Oh, I had a quiet patch, so I came by to have a natter with Annie."

"Oh, right you are. I'll pop back later."

"Please stay," Janet kindly urged.

"No no. It's of no matter. It was only idle chitchat," Cerys dismissed, backing towards the door.

She practically clawed the door handle as she desperately sought escape.

Cerys dashed back to the sanctuary of her shop, and shut the door of her inner sanctum. Her back fell against the door with a thud. Only then did she manage to start breathing again.

"Oh my days," she gasped.

***

Chen had accompanied Cerys to the shop first thing that morning to pick up some supplies on the way to the elinefae clan. He had taken Cerys' car and driven to the same car park Kiera had used for her jogging jaunts.

He shrugged on his large raincoat and popped his umbrella open. There was a fine drizzle in the air, which was somehow worse than actual rain. It stuck and clung to everything, and chilled him to the bone. His hiking boots squelched in the mud as he trudged along the paths into the forest.

Chen carefully approached the territory. He had been introduced to this clan, but he was still a stranger, and he didn't have the clan witch by his side today. He felt the tingle as he passed through the barrier. Within minutes, one of the Watchers approached him.

The Watcher wore a long Barbour coat and a wide brimmed waxed hat. Elinefae disliked the rain immensely.

"Greetings. I am sorry I did not announce myself first," Chen quickly apologised.

"It is good to see you," Pryderi replied, lifting his head so his guest could see his smiling face under the brim of his hat.

"Hello my friend. I am glad to see you. How are you feeling?"

"I fare well. But I am lonely. I miss her. Is there news?"

"Kiera remains with her father at present. There is a belief a daoi-sith may be at large, so I have come to add to your protection, if I may?"

"A daoi-sith?" he snarled, jumping into a defensive stance, his back arching.

"Yes. But be not alarmed. Her father and her own barrier are keeping them safe whilst they work out what to do."

Pryderi visibly relaxed.

"Will you take me to your Leader so I can seek consent?"

"No, I vouch for you," Pryderi offered.

"Very well. Please will you take me around the perimeter on your watch?"

Chen had already hoped a Watcher would assist him in his quest. He was unfamiliar with this territory, and he wanted to get out of the rain as quickly as he could.

Pryderi nodded, and led the way.

"Cerys told me her epicentre is the sacred space. May we start there?"

"Always that place," Pryderi muttered, shaking his head, but complied with the request.

The rain was falling more heavily, and a storm was threatening to break overhead as they reached their initial destination.

Chen quickly got to work, sprinkling black salt and clary sage oil as he walked in a circle, chanting as he went.

Reaching the centre, he knelt down and held his hands to the earth and continued chanting. As he rose he lifted his hands and spread them high and wide.

Chen had his eyes closed in concentration, but there was a bright golden light shining around the space as the witch carried out his ritual.

Chen asked Pryderi to show him the rest of the barrier around the encampment, and they started to make their way around.

Looking over his shoulder, Pryderi saw a fine golden trail. It was coming from Chen's feet and flowed out behind him as he walked.

"That is a nice trick," he commented.

Chen looked a little distracted, but replied, "Oh, yes. It is the magick spreading. Wait until the end." He winked.

The rain was getting heavier, making the journey hard going.

"Does it work if your feet are not in contact with earth?" Pryderi asked.

Chen nodded with a, "Hmm mmm."

Pryderi lifted Chen up and gave him a piggyback, also eager to get out of the rain. Much of the perimeter was unsheltered.

He started speeding up into a jog. The witch was getting jostled around.

"Wait," Chen called.

"Sorry, I thought it would be quicker."

"Thank you, but it is not pleasant. But it did give me an idea," Chen admitted as he climbed down.

He let out a long loud whistle. Within moments Shui appeared.

"My dragon friend does not mind water, and will be faster than even yourself."

Pryderi eyed at the red dragon suspiciously, but climbed up onto Shui's neck with Chen's assistance.

He grimaced as they took off. It really was the most disconcerting feeling. But as Shui wiggled on, Pryderi started to get used to the feeling. It wasn't uncomfortable.

The males both dipped their heads as the rain pelted their faces. Pryderi held his hat on and down, and ducked behind Chen's shoulders. But Chen had no protection at all; his umbrella would have been useless in the wind.

Pryderi started to relax enough to point out the boundary line. Looking over his shoulder, he saw the golden magickal glow in their wake.

Shui flew as quickly as he dared in the rain. He didn't mind at all, and was enjoying stretching his wings. But he was aware his companion wasn't of the same opinion, so took care to moderate his speed.

As they continued their flight, Pryderi became accustomed to the unusual sensation. The rain eased and he was able to view his home as he'd never seen it before.

The elinefae territory was vast, but from up here it seemed small. He gazed upon the trees and valley as they zoomed past. He could even see beyond his boundary; somewhere he seldom ventured.

There were so many shades of green, and they all blended seamlessly in a palette created by nature. The scene far below them was breathtakingly beautiful even in the grey murk which lingered.

Shui's wafting movements brought the scent of the forest up to Pryderi's nose. The petrichor and pines were even clearer and fresher up here. He breathed in deeply, soaking up every available odour.

For a moment the troubled elinefae forgot his woes and revelled in this wondrous sensation. He truly felt the beauty of his home. He felt it with every fibre of his being. He felt free.

As they completed their circuit, the air began to rush past their faces with greater force. Pryderi's stomach lurched as Shui began his descent to the sacred space he was guided to.

As they spiralled down, down, down. Pryderi feared his first meal was going to come up, up, up. He was incredibly grateful to feel the thump, thump, thump of Shui's feet hitting the ground as he came in to land.

The dragon only took a few steps to steady his balance as he landed. Coming to a complete halt, Shui bent his knees to lower himself so his passengers could disembark.

Pryderi was the first to slide down the red scales. He felt relieved to be on solid ground again, but was not so ungrateful as to forget to thank his steed. He patted Shui's neck, much as one would pat a horse.

The dragon snorted and dipped his head from side to side in his way of grinning. He had enjoyed the flight very much. He'd been cooped up in the small pond too long, and it had been lovely to soar through the sky again.

Chen was busy waving his arms around and chanting. A clapping sound echoed around the clearing as he brought his palms together high above his head.

The golden light Pryderi had seen trailing behind seemed to converge above the witch before bursting out like a firework. As the sparkling light fell, Pryderi saw a large golden arc stretching out high above them, which then spread all around. It spanned the entire boundary, creating a sort of dome.

This was the barrier they could always feel if they crossed its line. But this was the first time Pryderi had seen it with his own eyes. The golden light fizzled and faded. Chen's shoulders slumped. Pryderi offered his arm to support him.

"Come, we will get you refreshment," Pryderi offered.

"You can go to find food too," Chen told Shui, who immediately flew off to replenish his own energy levels.

The two males walked slowly and quietly through the drizzle to the eating area. Chen leaned on the elinefae's sturdy waist for support. Pryderi heard a loud grumbling noise, affirming he was making the right choice for his hungry friend.

Chapter 12 – Shui Makes Friends

As the boys found their own subsistence Shui was in search of his.

Having been on his short jaunt he didn't want to stop, and yearned for the big water. The fresh water pond was all very well and good, but he wanted to taste the sweet salty tang of the ocean.

Maybe it was meeting with the strong, funny elinefae his companion called Pryderi which put her in his mind, or perhaps it was some deeper connection. Whatever it was, the dragon followed the pull, and crossed realms to travel quickly to where he knew Kiera to be.

As he popped back into her realm on his flight path he saw a most welcome sight. He glided past the home of Threaris, Kiera could wait, as he sensed no urgency from her. Soaring onwards and over the cliffs, before nosediving into the cool, deep blue sea.

Shui blew bubbles through his nostrils as he rose to the surface. Launching high into the air, he spun in a spiral, before diving back down into the depths of the watery larder.

The next time he surfaced it was with a mouthful of fish. His tail was swishing wildly in contentment.

A strange being approached, making him pause his chomping. He peered at her through his large black eyes. Sensing no immediate threat, he snuffled and resumed his fishy feast.

The strange female with hair as red as the dragon's scales approached with caution. She was curious about the creature in her domain. Gradually swimming closer inch by inch, she kept her eyes on the creature.

Shui gulped down the remnants of his mouthful of lunch, and stared back warily.

"Hello, and who might you be?" she asked.

Shui's long thick lashes blinked slowly.

'*I am Shui,*' she saw in her mind's eye.

Much like the elinefae, the inner language of dragons largely involves images.

"Nice to meet you. I am Zondra," she replied.

The dragon emitted a sort of burbling noise of acceptance.

"How come you be here in my waters?" she enquired.

Zondra's eyes widened as he showed her the image of his young lady friend with long brown hair and green cat-like eyes.

"You are friends with Kiera?"

This time he showed her images of himself with Chen, Cerys and Kiera.

"Ah, I see. You are friends of friends," she smiled.

More burbling was produced. Shui was very happy this personage could understand him. He had not encountered many in this realm who could. Although he was telepathic, not all telepaths seemed able to hear his messages here.

Shui cocked his head to one side, and sent Zondra images of him chasing shoals of fish.

"It is very nice of you to ask. Yes, you may have your fill. I would not wish a friend of Kiera's to go hungry."

Again, he repeated his head tilt and sent her an image of Kiera, on her own this time.

"Yes, she is my friend too. I miss her," she added, her mouth turning down.

Shui offered her images of her riding on his back as they zoomed through the waves.

"Oh, that looks fun. Some other time perhaps? I do not like to linger here."

Shui cocked his head, but said nothing.

"I sense a great darkness. It frightens me. But Kiera is here and I try to check that she is safe."

Shui cooed at her. Forcing a smile, Zondra bid the dragon farewell before swimming off into the distance.

Dragons are simple creatures. He did not dwell on the curious female he had just encountered. He was still hungry, so returned to fishing.

Once he was full up he let himself float on the rippling waves and breathed in the ozone. Each section of his long body rose and fell with each undulation.

Feeling replete, Shui eventually forced himself to fly up to the top of the cliffs. Flying around the barrier Kiera had created, he concentrated on locating any dark energy which may be lingering. Zondra's words had made him cautious. He hadn't noticed a dark presence before, but hadn't been looking for one. And the sea had been beckoning.

A loud, eardrum piercing shriek burst forth as Shui discovered his target. Some shrubs in the cliffs were left smouldering in the wake of his fire burst.

He didn't hit the dark being below him, but hadn't intended to. His warning shot succeeded and the being disappeared from the area. That was good enough for now, until he could learn more.

He'd had to search for that daoi-sith. It had been cleverly concealed. No wonder he'd not noticed it before. This was reason enough to distrust the being.

Swooshing down, he landed on what could be called Threaris' lawn. Kiera's barrier offered no resistance to him.

A rather worried butler had witnessed this spectacle and informed his master, who in turn sent for his daughter. Kiera hadn't seen her father since he'd gone scurrying off the previous day. She was busily searching books in the library in an attempt to formulate a plan.

Threaris had retired to his own rooms. He was scheming, not researching as he'd told his daughter. The truth was, he was fairly sure which particular daoi-sith was haunting him. He was plotting his revenge, and trying to prepare himself so he'd not be so easily ensnared this time.

Jeffers now hurriedly led Kiera to her father's rooms, and stood quietly to one side, in case he was needed. Threaris raised an inquisitive eyebrow at Kiera, and indicated the image in the water bowl before him.

"Does this belong to you?" he enquired with a wry look.

Kiera looked at the image and gasped as she saw Shui.

"No. He is Chen's familiar. I will go out and greet him. Maybe something's happened?"

Before Threaris could respond, she transported herself outside, her magick taking her to the dragon in the blink of an eye.

"Hello cutie," Kiera hailed as she reached out her hand.

Shui stretched out his neck and dipped his head side to side, making a sort of deep purring noise. Kiera stroked the dragon's scaly muzzle.

His mouth formed an 'o' shape just before he shrank down to the same height as the sorceress.

Kiera laughed, and rubbed his neck. "That's better. Hello. Is everyone OK?"

Kiera was shown snapshots of Pryderi's flying experience.

"Oh, that looks fun," she exclaimed.

Shui showed her the improved shield over the elinefae Chen created.

"Ah, OK. Well, I'm glad he's safe."

Kiera plonked her bum down on the grass, and leant her head against her dragon companion.

"Oh, I miss him, Shui," she sighed.

She heard a sort of whine next to her.

"Miss who?" her father asked, walking over.

"Pryderi."

"Well, bring him here. I don't know why you didn't do so already. He is welcome."

Kiera rolled her eyes and sighed as she ran her hand over her forehead.

"Nobody told you?"

"Tell me what?"

Kiera regaled him with her whole sorry story, with her father sitting patiently next to her.

"My dear, why did you not tell me at once?" Threaris reprimanded her.

"I didn't really have the chance."

"I suppose events have overcome us. I am sorry," he sympathised, putting his arm around her shoulders.

It was the final straw. She'd managed to hold herself together until that simple act of kindness. Sobs breached her defences.

Her father held her to his side, whilst long dragony nose nudged her other arm. Kiera swiped the tears off her face, and took some deep breaths whilst mumbling apologies.

"We need to do something about this," Threaris said, patting Kiera's hand.

"But perhaps we should go inside to discuss this. I fear we have loitered too long out here," he added, glancing around nervously.

He and Kiera heard a snort. Their heads turned to see a small puff of smoke coming from a rather smug looking dragon. Kiera was shown Shui's fiery assault at their enemy, and she relayed the information to her father. This brought a chuckle from the sorcerer.

"A very useful friend to have indeed. My thanks to you," he said, nodding his head reverently towards Shui.

The dragon jerked his head up.

Chapter 13 – Intervention

The Chinese witch had eaten, and called Shui back for a swift exit. He was trying to avoid Rhion and feared he may not be able to do so much longer.

Although he'd now protected the clan from any form of dark energy, it did not expel any that was here already. Chen didn't know how to cleanse the Leader from the high levels of dark energy he detected in him from a distance. He daren't approach him directly on his own.

The witch's escape attempt was ill timed however. Rhion was stomping through the trees towards Chen.

"*What do you do here?*" the Leader bellowed.

"*My apologies. I was just leaving. I have enhanced your barrier under Cerys' instruction.*"

"*Why is she not here herself?*"

"*I have more practice with this magick,*" Chen replied honestly, not wishing to enflame this male's anger by admitting Cerys had to be elsewhere.

"*And why did you not seek permission?*"

"*Perhaps I should. Have done, but I believed it was not necessary and there was some urgency. Cerys believes there is the threat of a daoi-sith,*" he admitted, watching Rhion's reaction carefully.

"*But they have not been known for many a year.*"

"Even so, there may be one now. I have protected your clan to be on the safe side."

Their rather heated conversation was interrupted by a squawk as Shui came in to land.

"And now a dragon?" Rhion blustered.

"Shui is my familiar, and is here to take me away," Chen explained with a bow.

Chen did a double take however, as he saw Threaris and Kiera dismounting.

"Or at least I thought so," he added, a little flustered.

He approached his mischievous friend so he could put his hand on the cheek which was being offered to him.

'What are you up to, my friend?' he asked quietly.

The dragon just looked back at him with a smug squint.

Kiera noticed her mate in the forest clearing, and ran into his open arms without thought. Nothing else in the world existed to her in that moment except for Pryderi. She nuzzled in close to him, inhaling his juniper and sandalwood scent which felt like 'home' to her.

"I told you to stay away," Rhion roared at her.

Threaris stepped up to the Leader.

"And why is that? Why do you deny my daughter?" he asked in his most superior tone.

"She is not pure," the Leader challenged back, his lip curling.

"You dare say this to me, her father?" Threaris countered, staring into the Leader's eyes.

"I do. It is the truth."

"You need reminding she is part sorceress?"

"I do not. It is the very reason she must not be here. Trouble follows your kind," he snarled.

"And it stays clear of yours, I suppose?" Threaris asked, his voice chillingly calm.

"We do not welcome danger."

"You merely invite it by tearing these two apart. Surely you can see they belong together? Look at them," he said, indicating the pair who were holding each other tightly.

"*All I see is betrayal.*" Rhion growled towards his Watcher.

"I refused to truly believe it before I saw this for myself," Threaris uttered.

"Do not disrespect me."

"No, you should not disrespect me or mine," Threaris drawled, his eyes narrowing.

He looked over his shoulder as he called out, "Kiera, it is time for us to depart."

With shock, horror and fear in her eyes, she looked at Pryderi. She didn't want to leave him here with this male, fearing the repercussions from this encounter.

'I have your protection. You see I must stay. My clan needs me,' Pryderi thought to her.

She nodded her sad silent agreement and obediently climbed up onto the dragon's neck.

As Threaris turned to walk back to Shui he heard the dragon's warning squawk. Simultaneously, he felt Rhion's failed attack. The shield stopped any harm from befalling the sorcerer. A barrier spell his own daughter had helpfully invoked when she removed his access to magick.

Threaris calmly turned to the stunned Leader. If looks could kill, the sorcerer's surely would have in that moment. Disdain oozed from him like sap from a tree.

"Really?" he sneered, "You would attack a sorcerer? This is madness indeed."

Before he climbed up onto Shui, Chen palmed a necklace across to Pryderi when nobody was looking. A metal cross with a ball of jet at its centre hung from the leather cord. Pryderi accepted the protective charm with a silent nod of thanks.

"I am sorry for the trouble," Threaris apologised to Chen as he joined him and Kiera aboard the dragon.

Without waiting a second longer than required, Shui took to the skies. To avoid human eyes he flew between realms, only re-emerging in Cerys' garden.

The trio disembarked, and with a quick snort Shui shrank and scurried off to the safety of his pond, away from the complicated fleshy beings.

Chen, Threaris and Kiera went into the cottage for a well-earned cup of tea and some munchies. They'd all been silent on the short flight back, each reflecting on the chaos that engulfed them.

"What were you thinking?" Chen asked Threaris as he carried the tea tray in to the lounge.

"I hoped I could reason with the buffoon," the sorcerer replied with a flick of his wrist.

"Clearly that is not possible. What do you think, having seen him?"

"I could see the external influence, but without magick, I was unable to do anything about it," he commented, casting an accusing glance at Kiera.

"You are still not ready," Kiera defended.

"Perhaps," he admitted with a smile, "I certainly would've taught that moron a lesson though."

"And that is why you are not to be trusted."

"What would you have me do?"

"Nothing. This is my fight. I can fend for myself."

The two males both grinned at that. They had to admit she was more than capable. But inwardly, Threaris argued. This was his fault, and he had every intention of being the one to remedy it.

Frydah fizzed into view, and immediately began berating her charge, "Kiera, there you are. You keep hopping around. You disappeared on me without so much as a by-your-leave. I'm supposed to be protecting you."

"Hello Frydah," Kiera simply greeted the cross faery, with an amused smile.

"Well, at least you're safe. What are we doing here anyway? And why did you go to the elinefae territory?"

Kiera winced and massaged her temples as a headache struck.

"We are fully protected here are we not?" Frydah checked with Chen, mouth agape.

"Yes."

"So why is she hurting?" Frydah's query was accompanied with her hands on her hips and a mid-air toe tap.

Kiera yelped as she doubled over.

Threaris knelt in front of his daughter and commanded, "Look at me."

Instead of complying she squinted tighter and hissed.

"Kiera, fight it. Come on, look at me," her father said more firmly.

She groaned instead. Her hand went to her forehead, trying to stop the increasing pain.

"Gargh, I can't help without magick, Kiera. You have to fight," he told her, tapping her cheek.

She cried out whilst rubbing her head and gritting her teeth.

Frydah flittered, sending golden energy into the girl's aura, but to no avail.

Her father looked at Chen and asked, "Is there nothing you can do?"

But the witch had already lit a bundle of sage, and was smudging the room. He stepped closer, wafting the smoke around Kiera.

A cold sweat had broken out on her forehead, and she rocked herself.

"Against psychic attack? I thought it was impossible here. What else would you have me do?" Chen asked.

Threaris raked his hand through his hair. He refused to lose his daughter. Not now, not to him.

"Kiera, release me. It's the only way. You must trust me."

The girl was close to passing out now. Her whole body had slumped onto the sofa.

"Kiera, release me," he shouted, shaking her shoulders.

Frydah flew to the sorcerer's wrist. There were small golden sparks fizzling on his bracelet. She placed her hands on the jewellery and added her own magick to help Kiera release her father from his bonds.

The bracelet fell to the floor with a thud. Threaris' body filled with magick, sending tingles as it went. He breathed deeply like a diver about to jump from the high board. He let the magick consume him, and he consumed it. It was intoxicating.

Forcing himself to focus, he ran his hands in front of Kiera's face. He drew circles in the air before drawing his fingers in and out as if he were pulling strings.

"Quick, pour the remaining tea from the pot into the fireplace," he commanded Chen.

Threaris continued his pulling, circling, drawing movements. He brought his hands into a ball, as if holding something, and beckoned Chen with a nod of his head. As soon as the witch was near enough, Threaris dumped whatever he was holding into the teapot.

Frydah thought she caught the glimpse of some sticky black goo before Threaris put the lid back on the pot. He quickly sealed the spout with a tiny bolt of blue lightning which shot out from his hands.

Threaris positioned himself on the sofa so Kiera's head was on his knees, and slowly helped her sit up. Using his body to steady her, he picked up a cup from the table next to him and held it to her lips so she could sip the tea.

Once she'd finished Threaris moved so she could lie back down. She moaned at the movement but resettled herself. Her father patted her hand reassuringly.

Moving across to one of the armchairs he threw himself down, exclaiming, "That was too close."

"Much too close. I do not know how his powers reached through."

"Do not concern yourself. He is very powerful. I suspect he has a talisman somewhere. We should leave as soon as she can move."

"Bollocks to this. I'm taking her to the fae realm like I suggested in the first place," Frydah interjected.

"It may not be a bad idea," Threaris conceded.

"But Cerys did not want her to go," Chen reminded Frydah.

"She also said if the threat increased she'd agree. Well, the threat level just went sky high. And as for you, Mr Sneaky, you have your powers back, so I'm sure you're happy," she said, glaring at the sorcerer.

"You think almost losing my daughter to a daoi-sith makes me happy? What do you think of me?"

"I'm sorry. Oh, I'm just too worried," Frydah said, hands covering her mouth.

"As for the magick, yes, it feels good to be reconnected, but it also puts me in the path of danger again. Here," he said, picking up the bracelet, "As a sign of trust, I'll put this back on. You two will have the power to reactivate it should you need to."

"You doubt yourself?"

"No, but I do not underestimate the daoi-sith."

"Very well," she agreed, helping him tie the bracelet back on, and zapping it so he at least couldn't take it off.

"Who's sneaky now?" he gently chided.

"It's not that I don't trust you."

"Much."

"But I'd hate for it to become loose and drop off or get lost."

"Oh that would be a pity," he said with a grin.

Kiera sat up with a groan.

"That's our cue to leave," Frydah said, flitting over to Kiera.

"What? Where are we going?" Kiera asked sleepily.

"Somewhere fun," Frydah told her as she transported them.

"Bye then," Threaris said into thin air.

"Haha, she is a fine one to criticise. Disappears without warning. It is OK for her but not anyone else?" Chen observed.

"Faery," Threaris commented, as if that explained everything.

"They are tricky creatures are they not?"

"Yes, very tricky. I suppose I had better be off too. Thank you for the err...tea."

"Will Cerys and I be safe here now?"

"Oh yes."

"You are sure?"

"Quite. Thanks again," Threaris said as he vanished out of the cottage, taking the sealed teapot with him.

Chen went into the garden to check on Shui. As he stepped outside he heard some birds take flight, disturbed by his presence.

Chapter 14 – Illumination

Cerys had received quite a shock in the coffee shop, and even herbal tea hadn't subdued her shaking hands. She was fussing and bustling around her shop, grateful there'd been no customers since her encounter.

As she was still pacing to and fro, the door chimes clanged. Turning to see who had entered, she immediately dipped into a curtsey. Her hands still clung onto her skirts as she rose back up on trembling legs.

"Please be at ease," a wonderfully soft Welsh voice flowed over Cerys.

"Yes ma'am. Oh my goddess."

"For once you are indeed correct in using that phrase. But I think you already knew that."

"Y…yes," Cerys stuttered, dipping into another curtsey.

"Let us sit," the glowing figure in front of her softly commanded.

Cerys almost sat cross legged right there on the floor, but the glimmering lady gently guided her to the room Cerys used for consultations.

"You have questions."

"Um, err, oh, what do I call you?" Cerys stuttered.

"I apologise. I should have formally introduced myself. You recognise me as Rhiannon, I am sure. But here my name is Annie. You may continue to use that name to avoid any slipups."

"It seems so informal for a goddess."

"Perhaps, but it is my name so please feel free to use it."

"How have I not seen you before?"

"I had been careful to conceal myself from you. I am sorry for the secrecy, but I did not wish to cause alarm, as I regrettably now seem to have done."

"How has Kiera not noticed your glow? I know the humans will not, but surely she…"

"She had turned away from magick and had not transitioned. I fear she may notice should she see me now. Please warn her, I would not want her to be shocked any more than she has been already. As for the elinefae, their minds are easily swayed."

"But why are you here?"

"Why does a goddess ever go anywhere?" she replied with a soft smile.

"They go where they are needed, but we do not have horses here in need of you. Unless there's a change…oh. Not a horse. A different kind of animal who was changing. Kiera."

Annie smiled and slowly nodded in confirmation of Cerys' realisation.

"Thank you. Her transition was difficult. But you were here long before she arrived," Cerys thought out loud.

"Hm mmm."

"So she is not your sole reason."

A small smile played across Annie's lips, lighting up her eyes.

"Rhiannon, goddess of horses and death," she recalled, "Oh, it's not death is it?"

The goddess' long brown wavy hair swayed as she shook her head in disagreement.

"Let me see. Your aspects are change, death, fertility. Oh, is someone going to have a baby?"

"Perhaps, but that is not why."

"Err, dreams, protection. Oh, I give up."

"And mother of...?"

"Pryderi! Oh my goddess, is he?"

Annie chuckled, "No. He is not my Pryderi. But I confess his name caught my attention."

"As did his scent, I imagine. Pine trees are your forte, are they not?"

Annie chuckled some more. "Yes, but he doesn't smell so strongly of the forest that his scent called me. The magick in this area has been increasing for some time now. Where there is light there is also darkness. I came to ensure the balance between the two was not disturbed. Young Kiera has great magick. I fear this too has attracted the shadows."

"I sensed a dark energy too."

"That particular one came with the girl's father. A most unfortunate occurrence. All may not be as it first appears though. But I do not meddle."

"Much." Cerys slapped her hand over her mouth as she realised with horror she'd just scorned a goddess.

Annie was laughing though. "Well, Kiera was in need of a gentle nudge."

"That night she first kissed Pryderi you had a headache."

"Well, maybe I engineered my absence a little to help them meet."

"Thank you, I think. But are you going to remain here? I don't mean to be rude, but are you not neglecting others?"

Annie smiled broadly, "I like it here, and I sense I may yet be needed. I am a goddess. I can be in many times and places at once. Nobody who calls on me is ever neglected."

"Please forgive me. I did not mean…"

"It is alright. Do not be uneasy."

The goddess paused and excused herself for a moment. She walked out the back of the shop, leaving Cerys sitting in stunned silence and worrying about anything bad she may have said.

Annie soon returned and informed the Welsh witch, "Oh dear, it appears our young friend has travelled to the fae realm."

"Gargh! I was hoping to avoid that. But how do you know this? Sorry, ignore that, I'm being nosey and rude."

"Oh, a little bird told me," Annie said with her serene smile back in situ.

"Of course. But this is worrying."

"I am aware there was another attack on her. Perhaps you should go home. Your shop will not suffer from an early closure."

"Yes yes, I will go home directly. Thank you Rhiannon, Annie, ma'am," Cerys said as she stood and curtseyed again.

Rhiannon, currently calling herself Annie, wafted out of the shop, leaving Cerys to see what calamity had befallen her friends now.

Chapter 15 – Another Land

Kiera found herself in a magickal land. Magick was all around, and flowing through her, making her feel tingly and alive. It was as if she was breathing magick in like air.

The colours were all far more vivid here. The leaves on the trees were greener, the flowers at her feet were painted in a whole rainbow of colours. It was as if she'd been wearing sunglasses all her life and now they had been removed.

Gazing about her, Kiera started to recognise where she was. It was familiar yet different.

As if she had read Kiera's mind, Frydah spoke to her. "This is where I live."

"Oh, this is the forest where I used to walk the dog, isn't it?"

"Yes and no. In your realm, yes it would be. It is the same location."

"So the two exist side by side?"

"In a way, yes. More on top of each other really. It's not like walking through a door from room to room. It is more like lifting a blind and seeing the window, I suppose. It is hard to explain. I have heard witches talk of the veil between worlds."

"Yes, that makes sense, I think."

Kiera's nose twitched as she commented, "It smells funny."

"Different I think is the word you are seeking."

"Sorry. It smells different."

"Tell me what you can smell."

"It smells…sweet."

"Tee hee, yes it does. That is the magick in the air here. It feeds everything, making things smell sweeter and stronger. It is why we faeries crave sugary treats when we come to your world," Frydah giggled.

"Ohhh, that's why you eat so much sugar."

"Uh uh," the faery nodded happily.

"You're different here too," Kiera said, squinting at her friend.

Frydah fluttered her wings, cocking one leg behind her flirtatiously. Kiera could see a shower of little golden sparkles falling from Frydah's wings.

"Oh, it's like pixie dust," Kiera exclaimed excitedly.

"Faery dust," Frydah corrected with a sniff.

"Sorry, I have heard it called pixie dust."

"Hmph, I know of the source of this name. It is not a good book, Kiera. Faeries die in that story."

"But they come back to life when children clap their hands."

"Pah, as if humans had the power of life and death over faeries. The very notion."

"Alright, keep your wings on."

Kiera stiffened as she heard a snort behind her. Her reaction made the cheerful faery laugh more.

"It's OK, it's only Roger."

Kiera slowly turned around, but jumped back when she saw a large white unicorn right behind her. She only just managed to stay on her feet. This of course forced more laughter from Frydah.

Roger looked slightly less amused and was shaking his magnificent white head, making his brilliant white mane sway bedazzlingly. He emitted another snort with his movement, but this one sounded more derisory.

"Sorry Roger, this is Kiera. She's not met a unicorn before," Frydah apologised on her friend's behalf.

"Apparently," came the rather bored answer.

Kiera gasped, "Holy cow, he can talk."

"Hush you silly girl. Of course he can talk. And he's a unicorn, not a cow."

"I can see he's a unicorn, I didn't mean he was…oh never mind."

"I am right here, and I can hear you very well," he reminded them.

"Right. Sorry sir," Kiera apologised awkwardly whilst staring.

"And *this* is the daughter of Threaris?" the unicorn asked incredulously.

"Oh yes," Frydah confirmed, nodding.

"How disappointing."

"Hey," Kiera interjected, "It's not my fault I've never met a unicorn before. I'm sorry if I was a little surprised."

"I have never met a half sorceress half elinefae before, but I am not staring or starting."

"Actually you are staring a little," Kiera retorted sassily.

"I am? Oh I do apologise."

"You're forgiven. It is only natural to be curious," she said, smiling.

"Brrrr, maybe we should begin again. I am Roger, guardian of this area of the fae realm," he said, bowing his head with his left hoof stretched forwards.

"It is a pleasure to meet you, Roger. I am Kiera, daughter of Threaris, Sinead and I suppose Cailean," Kiera introduced herself with a curtsey, only now acknowledging the oddity of her tri-parentage.

"So, are we allowed entry?" Frydah asked, twisting her mouth.

Stretching into another bow Roger assented.

"Am I...would it be alright for me to stroke you, please?" Kiera asked the unicorn.

Roger looked a little startled at the question but seemed to shrug as he replied, "I suppose so."

Kiera tentatively stretched out her hand to pat the unicorn's neck, sweeping under his long mane. Meeting no resistance, she circled round to stroke his long nose. This made Roger close his eyes and breathe out through his nose in a soft snort.

"There, does that feel nice?"

Receiving no response she couldn't resist planting a kiss on his velvety soft muzzle.

"Well I never," Roger exclaimed, stepping back in alarm.

Frydah quickly grabbed Kiera's hand and hurried her through an arched doorway.

"What? What did I do?" Kiera questioned as she was pulled into a new forested area.

The trees were denser here. The whole area seemed filled with green foliage.

"Roger is a unicorn. A UNICORN, not a horse. He is from an entirely different realm, one which carries a higher purpose. Please try to show more respect."

"I'm sorry. I didn't know."

"The pointy horn on his head was a clue."

"Argh, I meant I didn't know how to treat him. And his muzzle was so tempting."

"Do contain your silly impulses. And he doesn't really speak, not how you think you hear him. There's so many languages spoken by all the fae that there's a translation spell in place."

"It's all very confusing."

"It's quite simple really."

"If you say so."

"There are rules here."

"Perhaps you'd like to enlighten me?" Kiera asked, spreading her hands out wide.

"There's too many to go into. Let's just say when in doubt don't kiss anything."

"Oh, very helpful. Thank you very much," Kiera sneered sarcastically.

"Just try to be respectful to everyone you meet. That should keep you out of trouble."

"OK, I'll try. Thank you," she said more gently.

As Kiera's eyes adjusted to the dark green light, she could make out many different arches hidden in the trees. They seemed to be in the middle of a circle of doorways. Frydah took them towards one of them.

"Oh, I'm the same size as you. Am I smaller or are you larger?" Kiera noticed with surprise.

"We have crossed the magickal boundary. We all appear the same size here. It's hard to say who has grown and who has shrunk, we just are. We found it stops people getting stomped on. Consider it elf and safety. Get it?" she said chuckling, nudging Kiera's arm.

Kiera rolled her eyes and groaned.

"So where are we going?" she asked, ignoring the faery's feeble joke about health and safety.

"So many questions. We are going to meet some friends."

"What kind of friends?" Kiera asked, wary of being shocked at any beings she may encounter next.

"It depends who's there," Frydah said with a shrug.

Kiera duly followed the faery who seemed even prettier now Kiera could make out her features so clearly. Her blonde hair actually had sparkling golden strands, and her eyes were a vivid mauve. Kiera had mistaken them as blue before.

The faery's golden dress was really quite revealing. It was low cut across her ample bosom and sat high on her golden thighs. It had thin straps over her shoulders, with folds which hung low on her back, allowing her wings to flow freely. Her feet were bare.

Kiera looked down at her own clothing and noticed she was wearing her elinefae-meets-sorceress style green and brown outfit. Her green cloak was shorter though, sitting just low enough to cover her tan leather trousered bum. She wondered if she'd dressed herself like this, or whether the magick here had somehow adorned her in these clothes.

There was a clear path the other side of this door, and flower petals were strewn across it in a colourful display. Dense trees were on either side of them as they travelled along.

Music drifted as they turned a bend. It was sweet and lively, and unlike anything she'd ever heard before. It made her feel like dancing. Indeed, she began to skip along the path. Frydah's flight pattern had become bouncier too.

As they approached what Kiera presumed was their destination, she could make out voices and laughter.

"Oh goody, they're dancing," Frydah noted with glee as they rounded the corner.

Chapter 16 – Lady of the Dance

A riot of colours and beings confronted Kiera's eyes. It was like looking through a kaleidoscope.

There was an enormous ring of dancers. Frydah pointed out some faeries, including Freddy who had joined the throng now he was no longer needed by the sorcerer. There were also some elves, gnomes, goblins and sprites. Even a few leprechauns had turned out for the event, and they seldom socialised with other fae.

Kiera lost count of the others Frydah listed. Apparently these were woodland fae. Some of them were dancing on the ground whilst others flew through the air, but all were dancing.

There was an array of different coloured folk and they all wore different clothes. Some wore long flowing robes, some had very skimpy dresses or shorts. A lot of the fabrics seemed sheer and wispy. Even the clothes were different colours; some were bright and vivid whilst others were pastel and muted.

Along with this dizzying concoction was the light itself. Kiera couldn't see a sun, but she saw a warm golden glow all around. She wasn't quite sure if it was the glow of magick or some other light source. But she didn't have time to ponder the point.

Her faery protector was trying to tell her something, but Kiera couldn't resist. Frydah's words faded into the background as Kiera found herself drawn into the dance. Happiness filled every fibre of her being as she skipped with the beings who surrounded her.

Laughing, she linked hands with what she thought might be a pixie. She didn't care who or what they were. They paraded around the ring jumping and spinning in merriment.

The colours blurred and her head swam as Kiera swirled with the throng. The music changed, and now sounded vaguely like the old English folk songs she'd heard, but far livelier and more harmonious. She had no idea what instruments were providing the delightful sounds.

A rather forward elf danced very close to her, but she forgot to mind as the music compelled her to wiggle and writhe. The elf leered at her lasciviously.

Frydah fortunately still had the presence of mind to intervene before matters got out of hand. She put herself between the two and guided Kiera away, whispering just one word into her friend's ear, "Pryderi." That one word brought some sense back to the young sorceress, but she was still swept up in the dance.

Many were entranced by her, and whirled her around in circles. Kiera laughed through it all, completely unaware of the power she wielded. She'd never felt this happy.

Little did Kiera know this particular dance was being held in her honour. Rumours of this unique magickal hybrid had spread across their land like a whisper on the breeze.

Little did she know that the energy of the music was building with her very presence, spurring them on to new heights of frenzied festivity.

The golden light dimmed and gave way to the most glorious pinks and purples in what Kiera guessed must be sunset. She had no idea of time in this strange place, but she thought hours must have passed. Shrugging off the idea, she continued her joyous revelry.

Round and round they twirled, on and on they danced, the rhythm and volume increasing with each song. They were stomping and clapping, jumping and whooping.

Suddenly all fell silent and still as a fanfare played.

All fell to one knee with lowered heads as a unicorn plodded into the clearing.

"Is that Roger?" Kiera squealed.

The deathly hush seemed to echo with her stupid question.

"Shh," Frydah silenced her silly friend.

"There's more than one unicorn you know," she added on a whisper.

All eyes were still focussed on the ground. The sound of hooves gently thudding against the compacted ground were definitely approaching her, so Kiera glanced up

"Hello again," Roger greeted, evidently amused.

"See, it *is* him," Kiera gloated.

But she was silenced by the majestic being who effortlessly slid down from her side saddle perch on Roger's back. Kiera had wondered why they were all bowing down for the unicorn, and had begun to fear she'd really not shown anywhere near the required level of respect for him.

Kiera felt as if her whole body had turned to jelly, it was quivering so much under the scrutiny of this supreme being.

The figure was willowy and moved with an easy regal grace as she sauntered towards Kiera. Her long white wispy robes wafted with her. Her skin was pearlescent white and seemed to radiate a white glow around her.

Her long white hair was adorned with a sparkling clear crown which Kiera wanted to say was made from diamonds, but it was more spectacular than that.

Long white, almost transparent wings hung down her back. Kiera smiled as she noticed pointy ears much like her own were peeking out of the female's beautiful silky smooth hair. The lady's lips were silver as were her eyes which were now glimmering down at her kindly.

"Greetings. You must be Kiera," she said, her voice slow and smooth like a Native American flute.

"Yes, ma'am," Kiera admitted, her head and gaze finally looking back down.

"I am very pleased to meet you. I have heard so much about you."

"Only good things, I hope," Kiera quipped before she could stop herself.

"Only good," the lady said with a smile.

Kiera felt like the sun itself was beaming blessings upon her with that smile.

"I am Una, Queen of the Faeries."

"I am honoured," Kiera said, hoping that was the appropriate thing to say.

She couldn't believe what she was seeing. There really was a queen of faeries? And she was speaking to her? Of all the curious, bewildering and confusing things Kiera had been shown, Una was top of the list. Kiera's mouth was hanging open a little as she began gawking again.

"Please come with me. I would have an audience with you," Una said, her arm gliding across, indicating the way.

Kiera managed to find her feet with Frydah's assistance.

"Ah Frydah, you may attend upon me too," Una assented.

"Thank you M'lady," Frydah murmured as she dipped into a curtsey, golden glitter flurrying from her flapping wings.

The crowd parted, allowing the three females passage to the doorway which had just appeared in a tree trunk. Kiera blinked at its sudden appearance, but quietly followed as she was bid.

She had expected to see some sort of wooden tree innards but found herself in a great white corridor with large white doors lining either side. Their majestic guide led them straight down the corridor, all the way to the end where it branched off to the left and right. Una led them down the left turning. The third door on the right opened for them, admitting them into a large room.

The entire room; the floor, ceiling and walls were made of an almost translucent white substance. It felt pure and serene, and Kiera was put at ease at once.

"I believe when this comes into your realm it is called selenite. Its properties change slightly when it does," Una supplied, seeing Kiera's fascination.

"I shall have to ask Cerys when I get back," Kiera murmured.

"Here, may I?" Una asked, touching Kiera's emerald necklace.

Kiera hesitated but let the queen remove her necklace. She didn't want to offend her by showing mistrust.

Una laid the delicate necklace on the floor and waved her hand over the top whilst chanting. Kiera saw the white substance rise up from the floor like a mist and envelop her gold chain. It wrapped itself around and settled into the gold, leaving the emerald untouched. The only visual clue left was that the gold seemed to glisten a little more.

Handing the necklace back, Una commented, "This will help keep your thoughts clear and your spirit pure."

"Thank you," Kiera replied as she refastened her necklace around her neck.

"Let us sit," Una softly offered.

Big fluffy white cushions appeared on a white futon which also popped into view. All three sat together, feeling very comfortable.

"You must be hungry. Let us have refreshment," Una said with a clap of her hands.

Trays of food and drinks were brought in and laid on low tables upon the queen's command. The sweet scent wafted around the room, and made Kiera's mouth water. It smelled exceedingly good. She was relieved when Una picked a few items and handed them on a small plate to her.

"I will leave your choice to you, Frydah," she said kindly.

Kiera and Frydah both moaned in pleasure as they took a bite of sweet jelly style treats. Kiera could taste roses and elderflowers, or at least that's as close as she could get to naming the flavours which filled her mouth.

Una hid her amused smile behind her delicate white teacup, but her eyes still glistened with mirth.

"You have been a long time in the human realm I fear, Frydah."

"Yes, but willingly, M'lady."

"Please call me Una."

"As you wish, Una. I am pleased to assist my friend."

"As I see. It is of no surprise now I see her."

Una angled herself so she could look directly into Kiera's eyes.

"Oh dear, but things have not been easy for her," Una commented, her smile fading.

Kiera struggled to tear her gaze away from the intrusive queen's stare.

"I am sorry, Kiera. I should have asked, but I feared the words would have been too painful for you to speak. Was I right?"

Kiera nodded, tears forming in her eyes.

"Please do not upset yourself. You are in a safe place here."

"But he is not."

"Oh, your mate. Would you like me to have Pryderi brought here also?"

"As much as I'd like that, I am afraid it would upset his Leader more."

"Oh fie, Kiera. A powerful young lady such as yourself cannot possibly fear the wrath of such as him?"

"I may be able to force him to allow me to stay, but if I did, that would be a hollow victory. I do not wish to live somewhere I am not truly wanted. I want to be able to find my home."

"And you still wish to make that clan's home yours?"

"With every beat of my heart," Kiera replied, her hand covering her chest.

"But the two of you could live anywhere."

"I will not force my mate to turn his back on his blood oath to his clan. And pardon me, but a house is not a home."

"I see the truth in your words. You are wise for one your age."

"I have been taught many lessons in my short lifetime."

"Indeed you have. And that must be why the goddess willed it that way. I am sorry it has not been easier though."

Una reached into a pocket secreted in the folds of her robes and withdrew a small white jewellery box.

"I wish to make you a gift. May it always protect and guide you."

Kiera gingerly opened the box. Her eyes went wide as she beheld a small white ring with a black stone sitting at its centre.

"I don't know what to say. Thank you," she breathed.

"Please do not thank me for this. I wish it were not necessary, but given the being who tried to follow you here, this and the necklace are apparently required."

"Followed?" Kiera asked, looking up with enlarged eyes.

"Do not make yourself uneasy. The dark one could not follow you here. Only light beings of pure heart may enter this realm. It is why this clever faery brought you after all," she said, giving Frydah a knowing glance.

"I cannot believe the daoi-sith even tried," Frydah commented.

"He has great power. Regrettably there is much darkness in that realm for him to feed upon."

"He broke through Chen's protection spell and almost got hold of Kiera's mind," Frydah blurted out.

"That is most unusual. He must surely have a tether."

"But Kiera has nothing on her. I would have known. I've checked."

"Who else was there?"

"Me, Chen and oh, Threaris. It's him. That daoi-sith must have had a tether to him. He was controlling him for so long."

"That would be my guess," Una agreed with a slow nod.

"And he used it to get close to Kiera. Oh that's just, just…"

"Evil?"

"Well yes. But does Threaris know? Should we warn him?"

Chapter 17 – A Magickal Duel

But Threaris needed no warning. He was fully aware of the tether, sensed it. But he did not remove the cursed ring.

After leaving Chen he travelled back to his home and evacuated the household. He didn't want anyone to be caught in the crossfire of the shitstorm he was brewing.

His daughter's bracelet was quickly discarded. The faery had only fastened it, and not empowered the spell. Her work was quickly undone, and the item plonked to the ground.

The attack on his daughter had been the final straw, and now he had access to magick again there'd be no holding him back. The daoi-sith must go. He would pay for the many years he'd manipulated Threaris. The sorcerer had been nothing more than a puppet for the dark elf for so many years. Well, he was a puppet no longer.

Standing alone on the lawn in front of his home, the wind whipped his dark blue cloak and the ends of his short brown hair. There was a grim determination gleaming from his green eyes, and in the set of his jaw.

Threaris placed the sealed teapot down at his feet. It was the one he'd taken from Cerys' cottage, and still contained the dark energy he'd leeched from the daoi-sith via Kiera.

Slowly pacing around, he drew magick in, arming himself. He knew the great power the daoi-sith held, but also knew his own power. And this time he would not be caught unawares. There could be no surprise attack now he knew of the daoi-sith.

Pricking his finger, Thre80is released the barrier around his home. His daughter had wanted to protect him. It was sweet of her, but he no longer required it. He was not afraid.

With a crackle from his fingertips, he released the seal on the teapot. Dark grey smoke began to seep out of the spout.

Thre80is knew the moment his enemy began to creep closer; the hair on the back of his neck stood on end. He had chosen the time carefully to allow shadows to creep from the cliffs and across his land, but there was still enough light left should he get into difficulties.

"Yes, it's here. This belongs to you, doesn't it? You need it. It calls to you," Thre80is taunted.

"You believe me to be a fool?" a sinister voiced sneered from the shadows.

"That would be unwise. We both know you are not. I openly acknowledge you have been very clever. It is not just anyone who can ensnare a sorcerer and have him do your bidding."

"Thank you."

"But you cannot deny the call of your essence."

"It is only a small part of me"

"But it is in fact a part of you. You feel incomplete without it."

The trail of smoke started to creep towards the shadows, but with a halt signal from Threaris it stopped.

"Oh no. You want it, you come and get it."

"And fall into your hands? I think not."

"I am here alone. There is no barrier, as you have obviously discovered," Threaris declared, spreading his arms wide.

"You offer yourself to me?"

"It is better to die than be your puppet."

At last, the daoi-sith revealed himself, stepping to the edge of the shadows. He was a thin little figure, full of darkness. His skin was a pale grey, his hair was white and long, but even that seemed tinged with darkness. His eyes glowed red as he stared down his prey.

"What are you waiting for, Donnagan?"

"That," the daoi-sith said with a sadistic smile as a cloud cast its shadow in the space between him and the sorcerer.

He thrust out his hand, and a dark purple energy bolt shot out towards Threaris. But the sorcerer was lightning quick, having anticipated the move. He countered with his own blue energy flow.

The two energies met in the middle of the pair, battling against each other, trying to win the tug-of-war.

"You really are an ungrateful little shit, aren't you?" Threaris spat between gritted teeth as he concentrated on his power.

"Ungrateful? What should I thank you for?" Donnagan spat back.

"I set you free. I could have killed you. I should have killed you on that battlefield."

"Yes you should."

"By the goddess, you mean that, don't you?"

"Yes."

"But I saved you. I saw goodness in you. You tell me now that I was wrong?"

"You merely stripped me of any goodness I ever had. You left me alone, the last of my kind."

"No. I left you with the light elves."

"They turned their back on me. They banished me."

The two energy flows were slowly drifting to and fro between the sparring duo.

"You had an opportunity and wasted it. That is nobody's fault but your own."

"How could I change overnight? I am daoi-sith. You were a fool to think I could be otherwise."

The purple energy zapped forwards, gaining advantage.

"An elf is an elf. You could have chosen to live in the light."

"Spare me the lecture of darkness and light living inside us all. They exist in greater measures in different people. And now only darkness remains in me thanks to you."

The purple edged its advantage a little further.

"I will not believe that," Threaris grunted, pushing his blue against the purple energy.

The dark smoke curled up from the teapot and into the daoi-sith. With an evil grin, he looked at Threaris, who was looking worried. The dark elf had gained more power than he had ever imagined possible.

The sorcerer was trying to contain his enemy. The daoi-sith was trying to destroy his; it made him the stronger opponent.

With a roar Threaris sent sparks from his fingertips as he gave everything he could in his attempt to neutralise Donnagan.

In response, the daoi-sith wiggled his arm and wrist up and down, which sent a wobbly wave out towards his foe, diminishing the blue's power.

"You're boring me, old man and you have clearly outlived your purpose. Time for me to find a more powerful puppet," he smirked, channelling more magick.

"Noooooo," Threaris screamed as he was hit by the threat and the purple power.

He was sent flying backwards over the edge of the cliff.

"That was almost too easy," Donnagan cackled.

***

Down below, unseen in the sea, Zondra had swum up. The massive amount of magick had alerted her. She'd feared Kiera may be in trouble so had come to her rescue. But on her approach she'd sensed masculine energy in action.

This had led to her worrying that Threaris was up to his old tricks. He was supposed to be banned from magick. Nervous of what may be above, she'd hesitated.

Whilst she wondered what to do, she'd overheard the two males conversing, shocked by the revelations.

Just as she was about to act she saw Threaris' body careening over the cliff. In the blink of an eye, she sent the waves up to catch his lifeless body, carefully lowering it to the rocks below.

She acted just in time, and ducked below the water as a dark figure with white flowing hair appeared over the top of the cliff. It had taken him time to skim across the edges of the shadows, finally hovering in the shadow of the cliff. He had to be sure of his victory.

'*Play dead*,' Zondra commanded Threaris mind-to-mind as she saw his finger flinch.

He was in tremendous pain so complied. The daoi-sith spat before vanishing out of sight.

Zondra waited, wanting to be sure the dark being was truly gone before breaking cover. As soon as she was certain he had actually vacated the area she went up to Threaris.

She sat on the rock, cradling his head in her lap, the waves lapping at her feet. Gently laying her hand over the scorch mark on his chest, she sent her own brand of healing energy to his injury. A hole had been burned through his shirt, and seared his skin horribly.

The sorcerer's eyes fluttered open, and he found a pair of royal blue eyes fixated on him. Zondra's bright red hair had fallen across her cheeks. She was even more beautiful than he remembered.

"Does this mean you forgive me?" he asked through grunts of pain.

"If you want forgiveness you will close your mouth and not speak," she replied tersely, continuing her healing work.

"Ah, I have your forgiveness, but you still have your anger," he grunted.

"Will you please be quiet? I am trying to concentrate."

The sorcerer tried to lift his arm to mimic zipping his lips, but was unable to. Both the pain and the nereid's hand halted his progress.

Zondra scooped up some sea water and trickled it onto his wound, making him grimace and moan.

"Oh you big baby. Those who cannot cope with the consequences should not play with dangerous toys," she reprimanded.

"I wasn't exactly playing," he mumbled.

"Did I tell you to be quiet?"

"You did."

"Oh good. I thought maybe I had omitted to tell you, because you're still making noise."

Threaris managed to smile through his pain, but held his tongue.

Once he felt the tingly sensation of her magick leaving him he allowed himself a moment to luxuriate in this intimate position.

He gazed up until he saw her eyes looking directly at him again. He sought their depths for any hint of affection. Sparks flew between them as her head bent down closer to his. She licked her lips.

The world seemed to stop as they hovered on the brink of kissing.

Threaris cleared his throat, and turned his head away.

Sitting up, he excused himself, "My apologies. As much as I would like to kiss you it would not be right."

"And you are to judge this alone?" Zondra asked angrily.

"And that is the reason why."

He gently held her upper arms, not in restraint, but to steady himself as he looked at her sincerely.

"That anger is still there. It is not right if that is between us."

It was Zondra's turn to look away.

"You know the truth of this."

"Maybe," she whispered out across the sea, unable to look at him.

"You know it was not truly me."

"Of course. Otherwise I would not be here. You would have been splattered on the rocks."

"Well thank you for the imagery. But yes, I know I would. And I thank you for saving me. And I am truly sorry for what I did. For what he did."

"That is who you were fighting? From what I heard, I thought he was an old enemy."

"Yes. Donnagan was the daoi-sith responsible for my imprisonment, and the atrocities he made me commit. But I am still sorry. And yet, I know that does not quell the anger you had felt was for me."

"It had already built," she confessed, still not looking his way.

"I understand. It is your nature. You cannot fight it. Do what you must."

Her head jerked towards him then.

"What? You mean this?"

He nodded and told her, "Better out than in."

"Then stand back."

Threaris transported himself up to the top of the cliffs opposite his house.

The skies went dark and the wind howled as Zondra gathered her anger in all its glory. Her red hair whipped her face as she stood amidst the waves.

Her eyes glowed yellow and her face grew menacing. She stretched her arms wide, and beckoned the waves forward with her hands.

"Come to me, your sister. Come avenge my maltreatment. Come to my aid," she hollered as the tide began to surge at her command.

Unleashing her full fury, she screeched like a banshee as she pushed the sea, sending it crashing against the cliff face.

The sea roared in an echo of the nereid's own cries as it battered its target. Wave after wave pounded the rocks punishingly.

Zondra beckoned more water to follow, and the winds swirled with greater force to whip up the storm under her control. She shook and cried with the force of the hatred flowing from her, which spurred the waves forever onwards.

The salty water smashed and crashed away. It started to take hold, and debris began to crumble. Having found an opening, the sea sought the cracks to chip away more, striking violently at the weak points.

Larger pieces of rock began to tumble, and still the nereid continued her torrent of wrath. Thunder boomed and lightning lit up the dark sky above as the storm raged on.

The waves were relentless, never tiring of their attack. With each rockfall it soared higher and harder. A large chunk of the cliff tumbled into the sea, creating a massive splash.

"Now," Zondra wailed wildly.

The sea eased back as if it were an animal readying to pounce. The waves moved far away from the shore, building its energy like a coiled spring. Only to be released as one massive tidal wave.

It hurtled towards the failing fortress with the velocity of a bullet from a gun, its devastation even greater. Windows smashed and bricks crumbled.

Piece by piece her prison plummeted into the water. She was destroying Threaris' home. The place of her former imprisonment.

Zondra exhaled with relief as the sea claimed its victim, leaving just a scar in the cliff face where the house once sat.

The skies cleared, and the sea calmed as she drifted listlessly towards the shore.

She limply pulled herself onto dry land, where she laid on her back on the sand, her arms stretched out and a satisfied smile on her face.

"Oh, that's better," she whispered, breathing in the calming ozone, the wind now a zephyr gently wafting over her skin.

Threaris remained on the clifftop nearby. With his arms folded he looked formidable.

'*Feel better for that?*' he asked telepathically.

"Hmmmm," she moaned.

Threaris appeared by her side on the sand.

"I'm sorry, I didn't hear you. Do you feel better?" he asked with a cheeky smile.

"Hmm hmmmm," she moaned more emphatically.

He laid down on the sand, bringing his face close to hers.

"You're beautiful," he whispered, reaching across to stroke a loose red strand of hair behind her ear.

She stared at him, her blue eyes glimmering.

Time stood still as Threaris held his lips invitingly close to hers. He held his breath as he awaited her reply to his unspoken invitation.

She took a deep breath in, inadvertently breathing in the scent of him. It was her undoing.

She brought her sweet red lips to his, unable to resist any longer. She passionately kissed the man she had known he had always been. The man she had sensed so long ago here on this very beach. The man who was now free and all hers.

Chapter 18 – Rough and Tumble

When Shui had taken off with his passengers, Pryderi had been left alone in the forest with his Leader. Just what he'd been trying so hard to avoid.

"*Again you have betrayed me. You've betrayed your clan,*" Rhion accused.

"*Me? There was no betrayal here.*"

"*You let that female onto my territory,*" the Leader shouted, stepping closer.

"*You were here too. I did not know she was arriving.*" The Watcher refused to look away from the yellow stare.

"*You expect me to believe she just happened to turn up?*"

"*You can believe what you choose. I had no knowledge. What I do know is I assisted Chen in protecting clan. I saw you scolding him for it. I know I am not the one endangering us.*" Pryderi banged his hand on his chest as he spoke.

"*You would dare speak thus?*" Rhion bellowed.

"*Yes, Sir. You have forced me to. I remain true to clan.*"

"*Have you?*" the Leader growled.

"*I am still here am I not?*"

"Are you? Your body may be, but your heart lies elsewhere. I see this."

"I cannot help that. My mate has been denied me. You denied her."

"And yet here she was, along with her father," Rhion snarled, circling the Watcher.

Pryderi rolled his shoulders, squaring off to the Leader as his patience was tested.

"I repeat, I did not know they would arrive," he growled.

Rhion was squaring off too, readying himself for the inevitable challenge from the impertinent Watcher.

"Was that a dragon I saw?" Arwyn asked brightly as he rustled through the bushes on his approach.

The ferocious pair span and glowered at the intruder.

Arwyn held up his hands in a gesture of calm.
"Sorry, just asking."

Turning to his friend, he said, *"Pryderi, there was a disturbance, and I could not raise you."*

Puffing out a deep breath, he replied, *"My apologies. Show me where and we shall investigate together."*

The two young males started to leave.

"We are not done here," Rhion rumbled, halting them.

"My apologies, Sir. But we should investigate. We cannot be too careful. There is a dark threat," Arwyn intervened.

"Yes, there is a great threat," their Leader snarled, looking directly at Pryderi.

He did not lose the meaning, but made his escape with Arwyn whilst he could. If he remained he would surely fight his Leader. Then where would he be? He'd either be victorious and become the new Leader, which was incredibly unappealing, or he'd be dead. That option didn't hold much appeal either.

Once they were safely out of Rhion's range, Arwyn slowed their pace.

"That was too close, my friend. Really you must not rile him so."

"It is not my fault. I have been trying to avoid him. It was working, but that dragon brought my mate and her father here."

"Yes, I know. I sensed their arrival. I came immediately in case you required assistance."

"You did? And yet you waited so long?"

"I did. What could I do?"

"Perhaps you could have helped me, brother?" Pryderi suggested, his eyes glimmering.

"And how would I have helped?"

"*You could have chased them off.*"

"*Brother, it would be a brave Watcher indeed who came between you and your mate,*" he replied with a cheeky grin.

"*Besides, I was curious to see what would happen,*" he added, his grin broadening.

"*You are an arsehole,*" Pryderi declared with a playful shove.

"*Come take it. You know you want it,*" was the antagonistic reply, also issued with a shove.

The conversation dissolved into a shoving match as they began combat. Eyes glowed and teeth were bared as they snarled with rising aggression. The males began circling one another menacingly.

Pryderi surged forwards first in his attack, but Arwyn dodged him easily.

"*You can do better than that,*" he taunted.

Righting his balance, Pryderi began circling again, staring down his opponent who was mirroring him.

Arwyn faked an attack, swerving when Pryderi fell for the trick. Ending up behind his attacker as he was wrong footed, Arwyn knocked him to the ground.

"*You're making this too easy,*" he mocked.

Pryderi quickly sprang to his feet, but Arwyn was upon him in a flash. Pryderi landed on his back with a thud. Arwyn sat astride his waist and repeatedly smacked his friend's forehead.

"*Where's your head? Are you a Watcher or a pussy cat?*"

With a roar, proving he was more panther than pussy, Pryderi launched himself up and forwards, sending Arwyn flying, who bumped his arse on the ground as he landed.

Pryderi launched himself at Arwyn. It was his turn to straddle his opponent. His fangs were bared and his eyes were glowing ferociously as he brought his face close to Arwyn's.

"*I am here where I have pledged to be,*" he growled, landing a punch across Arwyn's jaw.

Arwyn's hand flung up to his face. "*Hey, easy tiger.*"

"*Easy? What in this life is fucking easy?*" Pryderi hissed, not relinquishing his hold.

Not liking his friend's current lack of control, Arwyn decided to end what was supposed to be a play fight. He had been aiming to work off some pent up aggression, but this was getting serious.

He rolled, taking Pryderi with him, holding him in place with his hips, and pinning his wrists to the ground by his head.

"*Nothing is easy, but you do not ever take it out on friends,*" he cautioned.

"*You started it,*" Pryderi said, still looking wild as he wriggled under Arwyn.

"*Yes, and I'm ending it,*" Arwyn declared, planting a playful kiss on Pryderi's lips.

"*Eurgh, fuck you,*" he grimaced, finally wrestling his way free, but laughing as he did.

"*In your dreams,*" Arwyn teased, also laughing.

"*More like yours. I'm a mated male.*"

"*Yes you are. Not happily though. So what are we going to do about that?*" Arwyn asked, becoming sombre.

"*Alas, I still do not know. But I must do something and soon. I do not think I can last much longer here like this,*" Pryderi confessed, raking his hands through his hair.

'No you can't,' Arwyn agreed sadly, hoping he'd kept that thought to himself.

"*She was here. I had her in my arms, and then I let her go again,*" Pryderi raised his voice and hands in frustration.

"*She will be here again, my friend. We will find a way. We have to.*"

He did not add 'to save your sanity if nothing else,' as he feared was truly the case. Pryderi had fought like a youngling, had been distracted for days, and was really not himself. He hated watching the pain and frustration Pryderi was suffering.

Chapter 19 – Telling Tales

"You owe me a house," Threaris lightly teased Zondra as they pulled away from their kiss on the beach.

"Let us not keep score of who owes whom. It may be expensive for you," she smirked.

"I owe you my life. It does not get more expensive than that."

"I like this new you," she told him, brushing his cheek with her fingers.

"It is the old me. The true me. I am sorry you ever saw the version controlled by that daoi-sith."

"Yes, what are we to do about him?"

"We? You would assist? This is not your battle."

"Well, you clearly need help," she said, pursing her lips.

"Oh clearly."

"So, what do we need? We need to plan our attack. What will defeat our foe?"

Threaris smiled, and trailed a finger along her lips as he told her, "I like how we are we already."

"After that kiss I didn't even think that was up for debate. Now come on, focus on the daoi-sith."

"I think we need a little help from some more friends. Are you happy to come away with me?"

"No, I thought I'd just stay here and fight," she replied sarcastically, making Threaris chuckle.

Carefully removing the ring, he left it in a safe place on the beach, not wanting to take the tether with him. He had the element of surprise at the moment. Donnagan believed him to be dead, and he wanted to keep that illusion as long as possible.

Zondra looked at him curiously as he walked back to her. He planted a kiss on her cheek.

"OK, come on then," he said softly as he took her hand, transporting them to a certain Welsh cottage.

Arriving in the garden, they saw Chen gathering vegetables for dinner. The newly formed pair made their way over but paused at the pond as they heard a chuffed snort.

"Hello," they greeted Shui in unison.

Ripples formed in the pond as the dragon made his way over and waded out. He proceeded to enlarge himself enough so he could greet the guests properly.

Zondra petted the dragon's head happily, and was rewarded with images of what had transpired at the elinefae camp. She looked disapprovingly at her partner.

"Oh, what did you do?" she asked Threaris.

"What?" the sorcerer asked as he shrugged, trying to look innocent.

"Don't ask me what. You went to the elinefae and caused trouble, and you know it."

"I was merely trying to help my daughter."

"Oh yes, Kiera, where is she?" she asked them both.

Threaris was the one to supply the response. "She is safely in the fae realm with Frydah. She came under attack here so was taken away where she could not be harmed."

"Attacked? Here?"

"We are perfectly safe. The error was mine," he said, waggling his finger.

"Oh, that ring. He followed you."

Reality dawned and she squinted at him, "And you just happened to get magick back in the process."

"It was a happy outcome to an unfortunate event."

"You are a sneaky sneaky man, and you know it," she chided.

"Well, perhaps. But I did not mean to put Kiera in danger. She should have been protected here. He held more sway than I bargained for."

"You would not be here now if I believed you capable of purposefully endangering that lovely girl. But I have my eye on you," she informed him, still squinting.

"I only have good intentions," he promised, kissing the tip of her nose.

"Hello," Chen called as he wandered over, basket in hand, "I did not expect to see you here so soon."

"My apologies, but my home was errr…destroyed."

"Oh dear. Is everyone alright?"

"Oh yes, perfectly safe. I evacuated the household before inviting the daoi-sith for what turned out to be a very unsatisfactory battle."

"Unsatisfactory? You almost got yourself killed," Zondra interjected.

A squawk sounded by her side.

"It is true, and it certainly is not funny," she reprimanded the amused dragon.

Shui merely chuffed out a puff of smoke through his nose derisively.

"I think you had better come inside," Chen suggested.

Shui shrank back down a little, but insisted on accompanying them.

Just as they were getting comfortably with some calming, healing tea at the perfect drinking temperature, they were interrupted.

"Chen? Chen, are you there?" Cerys called as she rushed in.

The witch rose to greet her, "Yes, I am here, as is…"

"Oh thank the goddess. Chen, you'll never guess what just happened," she babbled, but then noticed they had company. "Oh, sorry. Um, oh."

"Come and sit," Chen said soothingly, guiding her to a vacant armchair and handing her his tea.

Chen hushed her as she tried to say something, and insisted she drink her tea first. They all sat quietly sipping, anticipation biting at their curiosity.

Only when she was finished did Cerys take a deep breath to begin her tale.

"Rhiannon, the goddess, she's here," she began as she regaled them with the details of her mysterious encounter, "And I really have no idea what she's planning, but surely she will help us?"

"You said that she told you she does not meddle though," Threaris reminded.

"Yes, and I told her 'much'."

"That was very insolent of you, by the way."

"Maybe, but it just sort of slipped out, didn't it? Well, maybe this could be one of those times she does meddle?"

"My darling, I do not think we should be calling upon a goddess to help with one daoi-sith," Chen rationally explained.

"Not even one who nearly killed a sorcerer?" Zondra put in.

"What?" Cerys asked, whipping her head round to Threaris.

"It is a long boring story. I welcomed a fight which I'd underestimated. It's all really quite embarrassing. If we could just focus on what we should do next, please," Threaris drawled.

"Fine, so do we have any bright ideas?"

"Well, first we need to locate the little blighter. He seemed hell bent on ruining my life, but now he thinks I'm dead I'm not sure where he'll be."

"Why did he want to kill you anyway?"

"It's an even longer, even more boring story."

"There is more tea in the pot, and we supposedly have some time."

"Oh, very well," he sighed, resigning himself to coming clean.

He poured more tea for everyone, trying to calm his mind which was a torrent of bad memories. Having handed cups out and regained his seat. Zondra's fingers intertwined through his. He smiled at her, silently thanking her for her support.

"It was the time of battles. It was a bad time for us all," he began, glancing around at the nodding heads around him.

"One clan in particular had sustained heavy losses. They had teamed up with another, yet they feared they were not strong enough. One of their witches requested my assistance. It was not my fight, but I saw their cause was good. They had been assisting the light elves in the desolation of daoi-sith, who had been running rampant through the chaos."

"The dark ones were terrible. They fed on the fear and hatred of those times," Chen recalled glumly.

"Indeed. As you are aware then, they are a difficult foe, and added to the melee. So I decided I would help at least remove them from the equation."

"That was brave," Zondra admired, knowing how difficult a task he had faced.

"More foolish than anything, but thank you. There was one particular battle. Most of the daoi-sith had been eradicated, and the elinefae I was with were winning the fight. The battle cries and screams were diminishing. I looked up and I couldn't see any land, just miles and miles of dead bodies and blood. It was a gruesome sight, and not one I ever wish to witness again."

"War is not pretty," Chen consoled, knowing all too well the horrors of the battlefield.

"No, it is ugly. I felt sickened. I had been part of the annihilation of so many. In that moment I decided enough was enough. I would not be part of such dreadful destruction. It was pointless, a waste of precious life," Threaris stated, the horror and sadness evident in his face as he lowered his head.

Getting sounds and nods of encouragement he continued, "And that's when I saw him. He looked so lost. All of his friends were dead, and he stood alone, staring at the destruction of his race. He fell to his knees, wailing like a child. I pitied him. He seemed to echo my own revulsion of what had just happened. I crept over to him, making it clear I would not attack. He remained on his knees and opened his arms, willing me to make the killing blow nonetheless."

Zondra gasped next to him.

"I couldn't do it," he confessed, hanging his head in shame, "I was called to duty and I failed."

"No, you showed compassion," Zondra urged.

He looked at her with squinting eyes. "You call it compassion? Did you not hear him yourself? He blames me for not ending his life when I had the chance. The merciful thing would have been to kill him but I was too cowardly."

"No, you are truly too harsh upon yourself. There is no cowardice in you."

"So what did you do?" Chen urged.

"I looked about us, and sure nobody was watching, I stole Donnagan from the bloody scene. I transported him far away. He looked shocked, as well he might. Then fear gripped him, as he thought I may be about to torture him."

"Only the truly evil can suppose the worst when they are rescued," Cerys murmured.

"It is what his kind would have done, so he suspected I had similar intentions. It was not his fault. Oh good goddess, you should have seen him. He pleaded with me, begged me to kill him without torture."

Tears were falling down Zondra's cheeks.

"The poor soul," she murmured.

"I assured him I would not torture him. I told him I wished to help him. Of course he did not believe me. He had no reason to trust anyone, let alone his foe. Only when I took him to the elves did he start to realise I was speaking true. But instead of being relieved he grew more panicked."

"The light elves are peaceful, but against the dark elves they were cruel. Why on earth did you take him there?" Cerys asked.

"It seemed logical at the time. My head was muddled with battle, I suppose. But they were close enough to being kin. He was the last of his kind. I saw a flicker of hope and chose to pursue it. I hoped they would look after him and help turn him to the light."

"You are truly kind to see the goodness where no other would," Cerys murmured.

"Again, I now see my folly. He made it clear to me earlier that they did not honour their agreement. I had reasoned with them, gave them my promise I would intervene should he cause trouble. They in turn promised to aid him. But I have since learned they shunned him instead. He was turned away, and was truly all alone in the world."

"But you were not to know," Zondra soothed, stroking his arm.

"I believed in the light. But they turned out to be all the darker for their pretence of it," he sneered.

"There is light and dark in us all," Chen supplied.

"Ha, yes, and the balance is not equal, as Donnagan himself has reminded me. Perhaps I asked too much of the light elves. Or perhaps Donnagan made it impossible for them to help. I do not truly know what happened. I do not think I would believe what either side would tell me."

"So, he turned against you. He blamed you for all the bad things that happened to him," Cerys stated.

"Yes, yes he did," Threaris said around a lump in his throat, running his hands through his hair.

"The one person who tried to help him," Cerys stated sadly.

"He does not see it that way. To him I prolonged his torturous life when I could have given him peace."

"But that is sick. That is a revolting way of looking at it."

"No, it is merely the way those in darkness would see it."

"You still do not blame him? After all he has done? It was him wasn't it, the one who made you do all those things?"

"Yes, Cerys. Donnagan surprised me in an attack, and took control of me. He hid in my shadow all those years, forcing me to do unspeakable things."

"And nobody stopped him?"

"Kiera stopped him," he corrected.

"But in all those years before?"

"They did not know. They could not know. He was very clever. He used my own torment to make it look as if it was all my own doing. He took advantage of my grief. Daoi-sith are well practised in that skill. My friends deserted me, and my servants fled except for two. Jeffers, my butler always had faith in me, he knew that I was not my true self. He tried for years to find a way to stop the madness."

"He sounds like a fine male," Cerys praised.

"Yes, he is the best. It was he who called for Althea's assistance actually. Sadly, even she did not see Donnagan's presence and effectively imprisoned me with him."

"Oh by the goddess," Cerys breathed.

"It is what it is. Kiera unwittingly freed me. She took away my access to magick, and as he was so attached to me, it also temporarily affected Donnagan too. Kiera raised a powerful barrier around my property. It meant he could not enter as he intended harm."

"She is incredibly powerful."

"She is my daughter," Threaris said with a proud smile.

"But why did you not say then?"

"I thought I could handle the situation. I have fought daoi-sith before. But it seems his many years with me have unfortunately taught him too much."

"So how do we kill him? That is what you intend to do this time, is it not?" Cerys checked.

"Yes, regrettably I feel I must."

"You gave him a chance," Zondra comforted.

"To your own detriment," Cerys added.

"Yes, yes. I know it must be done, but it still does not bring me any joy. Zondra, you have suffered by his hand, you know some of what has transpired. So many have died at my own hands," he said staring at his palms.

"And this is but one more. Your last act of mercy. And we will be with you. We will help," Zondra told him.

"I had vowed never to take another soul. I do not want you all to be dirtied with my actions," he said, tears forming in his eyes.

"You think you are the only one who has had to take life?" Chen asked.

"Yes, you must have had to face many horrors yourself. I would not add to your burden."

"That is my choice to make."

"And mine," Cerys added, "I am not exactly innocent myself. I have faced more than my fair share of battles."

"Thank you. I don't know what to say."

"Then remain silent," Chen counselled.

Threaris turned to Zondra, "So you are the only innocent among us, darling girl."

"You know this as fact do you, sorcerer?"

"Yes," he said firmly, taking her chin in his finger and thumb, looking deeply into her eyes.

"I might have taken lives. I am a daughter of the nereid."

"Yes, and you have a terrible temper. But you have not killed."

"There is a first time for everything."

"And this is not it. Please, I cannot do this to you."

"You are doing nothing. I have a choice too, don't I?"

"Please don't make this difficult. Please stay here. You will be safe. I need to know you are safe."

"I am coming with you. I will not kill, but I will assist you," she challenged, her blue eyes daring him to argue with her compromise.

A grunt by their side made them jump.

"And Shui is coming too," she announced.

"Yes, I know. I can hear him too now, you know."

"Oh, I hadn't thought of that. Fine. Well, you know then."

Threaris grinned. Yes, he knew. He knew when he was beaten. He knew this wonderful being would accompany him, along with the witches and the dragon. He knew he had somehow managed to acquire some very good friends.

Chapter 20 – In Dreams

"Something tells me your father needs no warning," Una answered Frydah's question, looking at Kiera.

"I don't think so either. He has his magick back. He'll know what's going on," Kiera replied, swaying a little.

"Oh, but you must be tired after all that excitement," Una soothed, "Why not rest here for a while. I will have beds prepared for you both."

"In the same room. I'm not leaving her side," Frydah insisted.

"But of course," Una said with a slow nod, and smile which didn't reach her eyes.

"Why are you being so nice to me?" Kiera asked through a yawn.

"Have I any reason not to be?"

"That doesn't seem to get in most people's way."

"I am not most people."

"No, I don't suppose you are," she commented with another yawn.

Una clapped her hands and a smartly dressed faery appeared. Bowing to his queen he swiftly showed the two girls to their room.

Despite her tiredness, Kiera gawped at the scene before her. She had been expecting a palatial room, similar to the one they'd just been in, but this was something else entirely. Stepping through the door, she felt a familiar magickal tingle brush over her skin.

Walking into a dark forest, Kiera squinted, and could just about see one small alcove in the foliage. Walking towards it, small golden lights glimmered to life, glowing dimly all around. Trees seemed to enclose the whole 'room', and in the middle was a bed formed from fine intertwined branches. On top of the bed was a large flat toadstool, which served as a spongey mattress.

Tiptoeing towards the bed, Kiera crossed a carpet of blue and white flowers. Unable to keep her eyes open any longer, she flopped down on the bed. Frydah pulled a thick blanket of moss over her sleepy friend and dismissed the servant faery who was hovering in case he was required.

Sitting on the edge of the bed, Frydah stroked Kiera's long, thick, brown hair, as she whispered, "It's OK. Sleep now. I'll keep you safe."

Kiera barely heard the words as she drifted off into her peaceful slumber.

Frydah however, was still alert. Summonsing a mushroom up from the ground, she sat in comfort whilst keeping watch. She knew better than to let down her guard in the fae realm. And the queen was a little too eager to get Kiera on her own for her liking.

The protective faery reached into her pouch and pulled out an energising sugar cube. Munching on it, she vacantly pondered its size; the sugar cube seemed smaller here. It made her wonder if she'd shrunk or whether it had grown. Kiera's own question from earlier buzzed around her head.

In her dreams, Kiera found herself deep in an enchanted forest. She had gotten up from her toadstool bed and picked her way through the wall of trees and roots. Her journey started off in a darkness not even her elinefae sight could penetrate, but something spurred her on.

Feeling her way, she tutted before whispering a spell into the darkness. Her surroundings were instantly illuminated with her magick light. A path led off to the side, but she couldn't see where it led. Her bare feet soaked into a brown moss-like substance as she walked.

Voices came from up ahead. Unsure whether they were friend or foe, Kiera crept off the path and hid behind a tree. She waited several minutes, but the voices seemed to get no nearer.

Plucking up her courage, she silenced her footfalls and made her way between the trees. Stopping as soon as she saw a gathering of beings ahead, she closed off her light less it should give away her location, and crept a little closer in darkness.

"But will she come through to us?" one of them was asking.

"Yes, she must do. The palace elf put the powder in her drink as he promised."

"So why is she not yet here?"

"She is not fae. Perhaps she is slower?"

Kiera held her breath, knowing they were talking about her. She knew her drink had been spiked, having become unnaturally tired after drinking it. But to hear confirmation from these beings she believed to be elves was no less terrible.

"But will she help?" they continued, seemingly unaware of her presence.

Kiera drew herself up, trying to make herself appear as tall as possible. Letting her white light cascade over her, she stepped out from her hiding place.

"*She* is not in the habit of helping those who drug her," she declared.

The elves jumped, shocked by her sudden appearance. They all tried their best to look meek, but that is not a look natural to their kind.

Kiera's lip curled at their false obsequious grovelling. They smelled 'off'. She took an instant dislike to this band of fae folk.

"Pardon us, but we had no other way," one of them said, squirming.

"So you could not approach me at the dance?"

"Oh no, we were not permitted."

Kiera levelled her gaze at the speaker as she asked, "And why would the queen banish you?"

"Banish? Oh that is a hard word. Not banish, no. But our presence at the dance was seen as unnecessary," the male explained, wringing his hands.

"And I should trust someone seen as unnecessary?"

"See, I told you she would not help," one of the females of the group said, pointing her finger at the previous speaker.

"I am still waiting for someone to explain why I should," Kiera answered, tapping her foot.

One of the males took a step towards her as he began to speak, but Kiera hissed and looked so menacing, he swiftly retreated.

"Apologies. We really do wish to help."

Kiera's jaw clenched, and she crossed her arms. "With what?"

These elves really were evasive. She was fairly sure no fae could tell an outright fib, especially not in their own realm, but they were masters in the art of evasion. Apparently, even when they were trying to speak plainly they couldn't help themselves.

"With Donnagan, of course," one of the females said slowly, clearly thinking Kiera was really quite stupid.

"And just who is Donnagan?"

It was the female elf's turn huff.

"The daoi-sith who tried to attack you," she said slowly.

"Oh, I did not know his name. How do you know of him?" she asked, narrowing her eyes.

Kiera wondered if she should make a swift exit from this infuriating place immediately.

"He was left unto our care," the female admitted, looking at the ground.

"Well you did a grand job of that," Kiera sneered sarcastically, throwing her hands up.

All this mess could easily have been avoided if these elves had done whatever it was they were supposed to have done.

All the elves were looking subdued. Their heads were bowed, and finally Kiera sensed genuine regret. But she did not let her guard down, unable to trust them yet.

One of the males swayed his foot in an arc across the soil, making him appear more boy than man. "He was too powerful, we were unable to contain him."

"You were to hold him prisoner?"

"You truly do not know?"

"Clearly not, so you had better explain or I'm leaving right now."

"Your father, the great Threaris," the male began after a deep breath.

"Great?"

"We call him this. I am surprised you do not. Never matter, your father rescued Donnagan from battle and brought him to us. He was the last of his kind, and Threaris thought we could turn the dark elf to the light."

"He did that?"

"Yes, you should not be surprised."

"I suppose I do not know the great Threaris as you do."

"We vowed to do our best, and we truly did. We even limited his power, thinking he needed time to adjust. We instructed him in our ways. We showed him what to do, yet he fought us every step of the way."

"Did he stay with your family?"

"Oh no, he could not be trusted. We housed him in a separate room."

"So, you isolated him, took away his power and lectured him. Yet you did not adopt him and accept him. You showed him no love."

"Well, when you put it like that, no. But what should you do with a venomous snake? We would not kiss it goodnight or cuddle it tight."

"No use now to dwell on that, I suppose."

"It would never have been to any purpose. He did not want to change. If he had met us half way we would have done all you said and more. But he fought, cursed, struggled and showed nothing but hate." The elf gesticulated with his hands as he told her all this.

"And then he managed to escape," Kiera said, cutting to the point.

"Yes. We are truly sorry. We did not know where he had gone. He disappeared. We were afraid, so we came here."

"Where he could not kill you."

"Just so. Perhaps it was cowardly, but you did not see him. He had already tried to take our lives when he was among us. We still do not know how he escaped. We regret deeply what happened," he said, returning his gaze downwards.

Kiera took a moment to absorb all she'd been told. A whole group of elves felt they were unable to combat the single dark elf, the being who had managed to capture her father, a sorcerer, for so many years. Chills ran up and down her spine.

"And Queen Una knows this? Why would she not want me to meet you?" Kiera asked.

"Because she knows we would give you this," a female said, sliding a glass vial along the floor towards Kiera.

Kiera raised her hand and sensed around the bottle.

"It is safe," the female told her.

"You will forgive my apprehension." It wasn't a question or a plea, but a statement.

"Of course," she consented with a bow.

Finding it was safe, Kiera bent to pick up the gift. "And why should I not have this?"

"Because it will help you to kill him."

"Kill Donnagan? Why would the queen not wish me to do so?"

The female elf shooed with her hands. "Hurry, she is rising. She is rising. She is a suspicious woman. You must return now, before she discovers us."

Fearing the powerful queen's wrath, Kiera woke herself.

"Oh, thank goodness. I could not wake you. I was getting worried." Frydah exhaled as her friend awoke.

"I had the strangest dream," she mumbled, rubbing her forehead.

Chapter 21 – Friends

There was a knocking at the door. Without waiting for a response, Queen Una glided in.

"Did you sleep well?" she asked Kiera.

"Mm, yes thank you."

"An undisturbed slumber, I hope."

"Yes. Thank you. I had odd dreams about my father, but nothing to worry about," Kiera replied, stretching her arms.

"Please do not concern yourself over your father. I have checked and he is perfectly well."

"That is reassuring to know. Thank you."

"So no more bad dreams," the queen soothed.

Kiera smiled weakly in response.

"So, now you are rested where would you like to go?"

"Oh, um, I really don't know." Kiera twisted her mouth.

"I was thinking of introducing her to more faeries," Frydah butted in.

"Oh, a splendid idea," Una approved.

"Well, we ought to get going, if we have your permission?" Frydah said with a slight dip.

"Of course. You know where I am should the need arise," the queen smiled.

Frydah took hold of Kiera's hand and transported them to the outskirts of a faery village, away from royal scrutiny.

"Phew, I'm glad to get out of there. She's really intense." Kiera sighed.

"Shh, the forest has ears," Frydah warned.

'She can hear us wherever we are here,' she continued mind-to-mind.

'Oh, but we're safe talking like this?' Kiera checked.

Frydah nodded with a smile and a flicker of her wings.

'Before we go any further, I need to tell you about my dream.'

'Are you sure it was a dream?'

'Can I tell you and we can figure it out together?'

Kiera divulged all that had happened in her 'dream'. Frydah listened patiently until she finished.

'Reach into your pouch,' Frydah instructed.

Kiera reached in, and her fingers tightened around a glass vial, making her inhale sharply.

'Uh huh, just as I thought. You were astral travelling. That's why I couldn't wake you.'

'But I didn't mean to.'

'No, this was assisted. I don't like that they drugged you before calling you, but I see why they did so. I thought Una was being a bit odd, but I don't understand why she wouldn't want Donnagan dead. Everyone else does.'

'Frydah, I'm scared. Those I love may be in peril. If a whole gang of elves cannot control that daoi-sith, what chance do we have? And even if we succeed we may find ourselves up against a pissed off faery queen,' she admitted, putting a hand on Frydah's arm.

'Now stop that, you're starting to blub. And there are no tears permitted in the fae realm.'

'But…'

'But nothing. Come on, happy thoughts please.'

'Why are you not taking this seriously?'

'Oh, I am taking it seriously. I'm just not allowing fear to creep in. We have not one, but two sorcerers. Well one sorcerer and one sorceress.'

'You're babbling.' Kiera shot a frown at the faery.

'Ahem, two sorcerers, two witches and at least one faery. That's far more powerful than a whole troupe of elves. And now we have this little bit of extra help,' she said, pointing to the vial.

'What is it?' Kiera asked, scrunching up her face.

'Magick.'

"Frydah, I thought I felt you arrive," a cheerful voice called out, "What are you just standing around for? Come along, come along."

Frydah flew into the outstretched arms of the roundest faery Kiera had seen.

"Colle," Frydah screeched as she hugged the male faery.

Frydah freed an arm to beckon Kiera over as she shrieked, "Kiera, come and meet the bestest faery in any realm ever."

Kiera shyly approached, but found herself swept up in two chubby bright pink arms.

"Kiera, Kiera, at last we meet."

Finding her feet, and steadying herself, Kiera emitted a weak hello.

"Oh well now, well now, where are my manners? Come along, come along, I am sure I have some very fine nectar wine. Let us get to know one another. I'm sorry, I've heard so much about you I feel as if I know you already," he babbled, leading them to what Kiera presumed was his dwelling.

They approached a cheerful red door nestled in the trunk of a tree. Kiera's stomach tightened as she remembered the odd palace she found herself in the last time she entered a door in a tree.

Trying to distract herself, she studied their host. He had bright pink skin, but long purple hair and wings. Happiness seeped from his every pore, which helped calm her as she stepped over the threshold to his home.

She was relieved to see it was much more what she'd been expecting. It was snug and lit by strange candles Kiera assumed were magickally powered, as they all seemed to be the same height with no drips.

The room was like the hollow of a tree, but surprisingly spacious. There were snug looking furnishings. A little window was at the rear, which overlooked some other trees with similar doors. There were several books lined up on the windowsill.

Kiera slowly turned, trying to take it all in. She glanced at the twig like stairs.

"Please sit, sit," Colle offered as he bustled around, clinking glasses in his haste.

Frydah's wings were fluttering wildly, and her legs were kicking against the sofa as she sat next to Kiera.

"Here, here," Colle said breezily, as he handed the girls beautiful glasses filled with amber liquid.

"To happy reunions," he toasted.

"To happy reunions," the girls chimed, chinking glasses.

Kiera licked her lips and closed her eyes as she tasted the sweet wine.

"So, so, why are you here? Not that it's not pure joy to see you again, Frydah. It's been too long, too long and you have been greatly missed," he said as he patted her knee.

"You have not heard?" Frydah asked, surprised.

"Rumours, rumours. But I do not believe everything I hear. I wasn't born yesterday," he said with a wink and a tap of his nose.

Frydah giggled at her happy, wise friend, but coughed as she became serious.

"In truth, Colle, we are in hiding. A daoi-sith was harassing our friend here," she confided, nodding towards Kiera who was happily sipping her drink.

"So it's true? I dared not believe such a tall tale. Oh dear me. This is not good, not good at all."

"I do not think he will be a problem for long. There are powerful people on the case."

"But I don't think U…" A hand slapped across Kiera's mouth, stopping her from saying more.

"Do not say her name, foolish girl," Frydah reprimanded.

"Frydah, where are your manners? Poor Kiera. She does not strike me as a stupid person. Is it her fault she knows not of our ways?"

Frydah actually blushed as she apologised, "Sorry Kiera. You just scared me. Saying her name will alert her to our conversation."

"My house is always protected from big ears. Many people talk about their problems with me. But even my shield will not hold against her powers, dear girl," Colle explained kindly, wiggling his ears.

"Oh, that's why she encouraged me to call her by name," Kiera wondered out loud.

"See, see. I told you she was not stupid. Yes, she would want you especially to use her name. You are new to our world. And you are powerful. I think she must fear you a little," he told her with a wink.

"Why do you say that?"

"She sought you at the faery ring did she not? Do you think she seeks an audience with just anyone?"

"But I'm not scary," Kiera said with a shake of her head.

"Haha, you have a good heart. But if you chose to use your powers selfishly you could become frightening could you not?" Colle chuckled, holding up a finger.

"But I shan't."

"Well, well, that is good to hear." His purple eyes sparkled brightly as he smiled at Kiera.

"We have a dilemma," Frydah interrupted.

"Well, well, come out with it. Out with it."

"Well, we clearly have a problem. This daoi-sith managed to control Threaris for many years. He obviously has tremendous power. It turns out the sorcerer had previously saved him and left him in the care of some light elves. And now he's been pried away from Threaris he seems even more hell bent on revenge. He managed to push through a protective barrier enough to reach Kiera's mind. Fortunately Threaris stopped him."

"This is an unusually large amount of power, even for a daoi-sith."

"Yes, exactly. Well, the elves and all of us have sadly realised there is no helping the elf. We need to end his life."

"This sounds like the only option to me. Yes, yes. He has proven time and again he is not to be trusted. He is a threat to many."

"But we've learned that a certain white lady is against this."

"But why should she be?"

"I was hoping you'd help me discover the reason. It simply doesn't make sense. And now I don't know if it's worth us risking her anger for."

"But can you afford to take the risk of the daoi-sith remaining? Which is the greater threat, eh?"

Frydah put her head in her hands as she moaned, "I don't know."

"There there. Drink your drink. Let us solve this puzzle together."

Chapter 22 – Distractions

Frydah put her chin on her hand as she pondered their predicament.

"Donnagan couldn't have reached her could he?" Kiera asked.

Frydah gasped. "Wash your mouth out. No. She is beyond any such nasty mits as his."

"Sorry, I was only asking. He seems to be behind every other weird behaviour."

"He certainly has had a massive influence over your life," Colle sympathised.

"Eww, eww, it only just occurred to me. Was he in control of Threaris when I was made? Is Donnagan really my father?" she asked, hands flapping.

Colle patted her arm as he softly told her, "No dear girl, no. Do not concern yourself. From what I hear he was controlling your father not embodying him. He may have forced his actions but he was not part of him."

"Oh phew." Kiera sighed heavily, swiping her forehead.

"There really is no mistaking your heritage," Frydah confirmed.

Kiera smiled and waggled her pointy ears as she said, "What these?"

"They're clearly your elinefae half. No, I was talking more about your powers. And there's just something about you. You look elinefae, but feel like Threaris."

Kiera beamed. "You really think so?"

She was beginning to feel proud of both parts of her lineage. People spoke of Threaris as a great and powerful sorcerer, and the elinefae were powerful in their own way.

Kiera held her arm against her tummy in an effort to silence its rumbling. "Um, talking of elinefae traits, I think I need to eat properly."

"Well we don't go about eating magickal creatures here," Frydah harrumphed.

"So we have to go back? I was just getting used to this place."

"I wonder…yes, yes, your sorceress side might just…let us go foraging," Colle offered.

The bumbling faery guided Kiera through the woods, and to a small waterfall which gathered in a glittering pool.

Bending down, Colle picked up a wooden bowl and dipped it into the water.

"Here, here, try a sip of this. Just a sip, mind," he told her as he held the bowl to her lips.

Taking a small sip, Kiera beamed. It tasted like honey and elderflowers, but fizzed on her tongue like Champagne.

"How's that?" Colle checked.

"Delicious. May I have more, please?"

"It seems you may." He smiled.

Kiera eagerly finished the rest of the bowlful.

"How do you feel now?"

"Oh, I feel marvellous."

"Not hungry?"

"No, the need to feed has completely gone. That's…"

"Magick?" Colle finished.

Kiera laughed. It felt so good to laugh, like she hadn't done so for a very long time, not properly. She opened her arms and span in a circle, eyes pointing skywards.

Frydah hid her mouth behind her hand as she giggled. "Colle, have you got my friend drunk?"

"Oh as if I would." He winked mischievously.

"What? Did you say drunk? Was that alcohol?" Kiera asked, stopping her spinning.

"No, no. I don't think the nectar wine helped in all honesty. I think I have heard humans accuse others of being drunk on power," Colle said, strumming his fingers on his chin.

"Oh, so a lot of magick, power, can make you feel drunk?"

"Exactly."

Kiera playfully slapped his arm as she lightly admonished, "Oh, you are a bad faery."

Colle treated her to one of his cheekier grins, which made Kiera feel even more joyful.

"I am a very good faery. You needed something to fill you up and this is the village's local supply," he told her.

Turning to refill the bowl, he handed it to Frydah. "You could do with a top up as well."

Frydah folded her arms and scrunched her nose in haughty dismissal, but it quickly faded into a smirk. She took the offering and sipped.

"Oh Frydah, you're even sparklier." Kiera giggled.

"Haha, so are you."

"What?"

Approaching the pool, Kiera peered down at her reflection. A white glow with green flecks shone all around her face. She looked down and noticed it surrounding her arms and her entire body.

She span around again, sending little white and green flecks flying, laughing. This time her companions joined in.

"Come, come. You have been miserable far too long both of you. We need to celebrate our honoured guest," Colle announced.

"Fine, but if it gets out of hand just remember this was your idea," Frydah said through bursts of laughter.

Colle flew as he guided them back through the woods. Frydah did likewise, and Kiera found herself gliding along just above the ground. Whcn she realised what she was doing she just giggled, too happy to care how or why.

Colle's feet touched ground as they entered the village proper, and he skipped, calling out to all the faeries who lived there. "Come, come. Come meet Kiera the elinefae sorceress."

Many doors were flung open and lots of faeries ran up to join the parade through the village, all shouting and cheering as they joined what resembled a conga line.

They all skipped and bobbed along to a large open area. Colle clapped and an array of small golden orbs glowed all around the space.

Mysterious music began to play, and everyone joined hands in a long line which formed into a circle as they began to dance. This was different from the one Kiera had enjoyed when she first arrived.

Some faeries took to the air. They didn't just hover, they darted around so quickly Kiera could barely keep track, almost envious as she watched their acrobatics.

The circle soon broke up into a rabble of bodies scattering in all directions. Kiera clapped and bounced along. Her heart sang as she bopped. The happiness of these people seemed boundless and somehow purer.

Lots of faeries approached Kiera and greeted her warmly. They asked her many questions until Colle batted them away.

"They're here to have fun, not be bored with questions. Off, off with you. Be merry in the dance."

Some faeries remained on the ground out of respect to their flightless guest. They linked arms with her and made chains as they weaved and swapped partners.

Frydah and Colle weren't far away in body, but seemed lost in their own world. Kiera wondered if there was something more to their relationship, but the thought was flung aside as her hand was pulled, forcing her to twirl.

"Use it, Kiera," a little voice urged her.

Kiera frowned, unsure what the faery was asking her.

"Breathe deep. You can do it. Take off."

Kiera stood still, closed her eyes and inhaled slowly. Tingles ran through her as she soared into the air. Her cloak swirled around her as she twirled above the faeries.

The faery who had encouraged her was flying by her side. "I knew you could do it."

She took Kiera's hand and instructed her briefly.

Kiera was soon zooming around like all the other faeries, like a caged bird released into the wild.

"Weeeeeee," she squealed, swooping.

Frydah placed her hand in Kiera's and they swept through the air together, up and down, over and round.

"I didn't know I could do this," Kiera chirped.

"Not all who fly have wings," Frydah chimed, "My wings help me steer, but they are not the source of my flight."

The girls chortled as they danced together. Colle appeared by their side, sharing their merriment.

The dance lasted hours. The trouble with being in the fae realm is that one rarely tires. The magick sustains energy indefinitely.

Kiera witnessed the same pink and purple haze in the sky again, and supposed this must be sunset. She found it puzzling that it never got truly dark.

But like all good things, this dance also had to come to an end. As the instigator, Colle was the one to clap and dispel the music. This earned him grumbles and groans, but the faeries slowly disbanded, making sure they bid Kiera farewell on their way to carry out their day-to-day business.

Chapter 23 – Transported

Kiera had let herself be lulled by the fae realm. All thoughts of her own world were a million miles away. Happiness and excitement filled her.

This was not her being selfish. It was the way of life with fae. The incredibly strong magick and the absence of dark energy creates a sort of enchantment, a deep desire to pursue fun. Laughter can indeed be infectious.

Kiera was having the time of her life. It was thrilling to meet all these different beings, and to be held in a field of love. The dancing just added to her exhilaration.

Frydah and Colle were standing close together, muttering quietly. Even Kiera couldn't hear what was being said.

"Could it really be as simple as her not wanting any fae life to be taken?" Frydah was asking.

"Well, we know it cannot be with evil intent, surely."

"I don't know anymore. I felt on edge around her, like there was something a little sinister."

"You've been hanging around the humans too long. You've become suspicious. No, no. There will be a simple explanation."

"Perhaps a visit to the elves would help? Perhaps they know something without being aware of it?"

"I'm sure you're clutching at straws. But if it would help put your mind at rest, perhaps you should go. Yes, yes. I am sure Kiera would like to see their home."

Kiera's nose was buried in a flower, inhaling its delicious rose and vanilla scent when Frydah flew over.

"Come on, we're going on a trip," the faery announced excitedly.

"Oh good. Where are we off to now?" Kiera asked as she was led away by the hand.

"To see the elves."

"But I've already met them."

'Shh, inside voice if you're going to say silly things. Those ones are secreted away. They won't be there. And you're not to mention them.'

'Why?'

'Just don't.'

"Bye Colle," she called as she was led past their joyful host.

"Frydah, at least let me say goodbye. There's no hurry," he called, trailing after them.

Frydah halted in mid step, making Kiera bump into her back with an, "oof."

Colle pulled Kiera in for a hug. "It's been a tremendous pleasure meeting you, Kiera. It has, it has."

"Thank you. I've had a wonderful time. I hope we'll meet again."

"Anytime you wish to visit you will be most welcome. Most welcome indeed."

Frydah pecked Colle on the cheek as they said their goodbyes.

The girls picked their way along a forest path, away from the faery village.

It became quiet all around them. Kiera was aware of the absence of laughter and happy voices. As her hearing adjusted, she heard the leaves rustling in the breeze, and the birds singing.

"Are we walking all the way? Why are we not transporting there?"

"For a start, they're not expecting us. And the elves are a cautious folk. They do not take kindly to people puffing in and out. They like to be aware of company on their approach."

"Is it far?"

"Nothing is ever far in the fae realm. Besides, I have a fun way of getting there."

"What?"

"You'll see," she said over her shoulder with a naughty smirk.

The girls fell silent as the continued their walk in the forest. It didn't smell of pine. Like everything else here, the trees gave off a sweet scent. Kiera was no longer surprised at Frydah's sugar addiction. Everything here smelled and tasted sweet. It was like she was breathing sugary air.

Three birds noisily took flight as the girls neared their perch. The sudden noise and movement made Kiera jump, but she smiled as she saw the beautiful birds fly away. Their presence and song had somehow been comforting. She only realised this in their absence.

With nothing else occupying her mind, Kiera wondered why she should like birds. Surely with her cat DNA she should think of them as her enemy? Perhaps the cat people had enough other genes to compensate? She shrugged. Whatever, she liked them and that was that.

Kiera hummed softly as she wandered, without conscious thought. It was just an outward sign of her inner peace. Frydah fluttered her wings as the melody filled her with bliss.

Eventually they came to a riverbank. The crystal clear river flowed freely and steadily.

Kiera, who had been bending over, peering at the water jolted upright as Frydah let out two short sharp whistles. Everyone was a similar size in the faery realm, but Kiera was still not prepared to see two large water boatman insects swim up to her.

"Come on, what are you waiting for?" Frydah asked, hopping onto the back of one of the swimming bugs.

Kiera stretched her arms out, trying to keep her balance as she stepped on. The bug's body dipped in the water briefly before resurfacing as it adjusted to her weight.

She staggered forwards as it began to swim. It was such a jerky movement she thought she was going to topple over. But fortunately, she was used to her elinefae body now and used her superior sense of balance to remain upright.

"Keep your flight skills ready just in case," Frydah said with a smile and a wink.

As the insects made their way downstream Kiera became accustomed to their movements, and began to enjoy the ride. The warm breeze tousled her hair as they whooshed along. It was yet one more exhilarating experience in this amazing realm.

The scenery began to change. The trees along the banks thinned, and finally disappeared. Kiera felt as if they were impossibly rising. Water did not flow up hills though. She shrugged, realising nothing was impossible here.

Kiera's jaw dropped as she saw mountains. They *were* climbing higher. The air felt cooler and even fresher up here. It lost a little of the sugary sweetness and Kiera could smell a floral scent.

Journeying onwards, Kiera could see moss covering some of the rocks. Shrubs began to appear further along. She heard their thundering before seeing the stunning waterfalls.

At last, Kiera saw some buildings a little like Japanese pagodas, yet even more delicate and coloured white and gold. Kiera felt a tingle, and the air shimmered as they crossed the village's shield.

As the insects drew them further on, the girls could see the elf village in all its glory. Many pagodas were nestled in between waterfalls. Shining crystal bridges linked across expanses of water. Rainbows shone as the light bounced off those bridges.

This place felt truly magickal. The hairs on the back of Kiera's neck stood on end as she inadvertently drew some of the power to her.

The water boatman boats stopped at a clear crystal jetty, and the girls alighted, thanking the bugs for their ride.

"Greetings to you both," a female hailed them with a hauntingly hollow yet light voice.

The female elf at the far end of the jetty was bewitchingly beautiful. She was slender, and elegance personified.

A simple circlet crowned her beautiful long blonde hair which hung loose down to her legs. Her large elf ears poked up through her tresses. Kiera smiled, appreciating how wrong she'd been to ever liken her own ears to those of elves. Theirs were far larger and pointier.

The circlet was similar to Kiera's which was made of woven twigs, but this elf's one was apparently made of the same clear crystal as the bridges. Small golden ivy leaves embellished it. Where it dipped at her forehead, there sat a small moonstone and two dewdrops hung underneath. Rainbows danced in Kiera's eyes as she gazed at the circlet, making her blink and turn her head away.

Kiera felt Frydah's hand at her back, pushing her gently onwards. Her feet had momentarily felt glued to the ground, and she was grateful for the nudge.

She still gawped at the lady. Her slender form was covered in what Indians in the human realm would call a lehenga. A white crop top edged with gold embroidery ended high up the woman's ribs.

The short sleeved top was complimented by a long flowing white skirt, with an intricate gold design swirling around it. A long white shawl was draped across her arms and across her back. The material was fine and almost sheer, similar to chiffon but more exquisite.

"It is lovely to meet you. I am Nora, Queen of the Elves," the magnificent lady introduced herself, her green eyes crinkling slightly as she smiled.

"Oh, pleased to meet you," Kiera replied with a deep curtsey.

She hadn't expected to meet with any more royalty. Kiera was bewildered. Why would any royal want to meet her? She didn't feel that special.

"It is good to see you again, Queen Nora. Thank you for meeting us. I'm trying to show Kiera more of our world," Frydah babbled.

"We are pleased you chose us as part of your tour. We have a carriage awaiting you."

"You were expecting us?"

"Colle may have let us know. He is such a good faery," the queen said with another smile.

"I didn't want to put you to any trouble, M'lady."

"Oh, it is no trouble."

The girls followed the queen to the promised carriage. It was made out of a giant green leaf, with a large, open, white flower petal housing the cushioned seat. But there were no white horses or unicorns. No, this carriage had two large ladybirds to pull it.

Kiera hesitated, startled by the oversized bugs. Somehow these were stranger than the water boatmen. This world was starting to hurt her head. Frydah came to her aid, and held her hand as they stepped into the carriage.

'There's nothing to be scared of. This will be fun,' she discreetly told her worried friend.

'Promise?'

' I promise.'

Once they were all seated comfortably, the ladybirds started their gentle walk. It really was quite pleasant. It was very smooth and Kiera began to relax.

They were pulled through the village, where many elves came out to cheer them on their way. There were bursts of flower petal confetti all around the carriage.

"I assure you this is for you. I don't usually get this much fuss made over me," Queen Nora stated.

"But I'm just me," Kiera deflected.

"Are you really still unaware of just how special you are, Kiera?"

"I suppose I've been ignored most of my life. I never really fitted in. It's a little hard to believe that I'm anyone important," she replied, shrinking away from the intense green gaze directed at her.

"You are unique. And you continue to grow in your powers. You make everyone feel more alive just by being present. You have a very kind heart. You are the first sorceress ever to cross into our realm."

"Really?"

"Oh yes. Most sorcerers have too much darkness to make the journey. Our magick would be too alluring for them, and may corrupt them irretrievably."

"But not me?" Kiera asked, glancing at the crowds and waving.

"This is probably a conversation we need to have quietly in the palace."

"The palace?"

"Oh dear, you really are new, aren't you?" Nora commented, not managing to fully stifle a small giggle.

"I am. And just as I begin to think I'm getting my head around it all something else comes along to surprise me."

"You poor dear. We will look after you. Let us take the shorter way to my home, and you can rest for a while."

The queen wafted her hands, and the ladybirds spread their wings from under their red shells. Their wings buzzed as they picked up speed, and suddenly they were taking off. Their carriage was pulled through the air, up to the top of the mountain.

Kiera squealed, first in surprise then in bliss. This was even better than her river ride. She had to admit to herself, that even though there were many shocking things she'd learned here, there was an awful lot more wondrous stuff.

Chapter 24 – Getting to Know You

The carriage swept around in a large spiral as it came in to land carefully in front of the palace. Only once they'd stopped did Kiera realise her ears were ringing. The ladybirds' wings had buzzed and droned loudly throughout the flight.

Queen Nora stepped down from the carriage with poise and grace. Kiera slightly less so. And Frydah fluttered her wings as she hopped off.

"Well, here we are, home sweet home," Nora chimed.

"It's beautiful," Kiera admired, looking around at the large beautiful palace.

It was white with gold accents, like many of the buildings in the village. But this building had many turrets with white and gold banners flying aloft. It was built on the top of the mountain, but oddly had trees growing around it. Kiera had not expected to see trees up this high.

Far below, Kiera could see as well as hear the many waterfalls cascading around the village. The view was simply breath-taking.

Looking back to the palace, she saw liveried elf servants lined up at the entrance. Queen Nora was waiting for her to catch up at the foot of the stairs. But she displayed no annoyance. She was smiling, waiting patiently.

"The king is waiting to meet us inside," Nora announced as Kiera approached.

"Oh, um…"

"You did not know of the king?"

"I confess I did not," Kiera answered, blushing deeply and fidgeting.

"And why would you? You are new. Please do not worry so. My, you are nervous, aren't you?" she added with a giggle, making her way up the steps.

"I am afraid I may offend."

The large oak doors were opened, and the trio walked through. Queen Nora put her hand lightly on Kiera's upper arm, making her pause.

Looking into the girl's bright green eyes, Nora affirmed, "Please ask me any question in your mind."

Kiera bit her lip and glanced at Frydah who just nodded.

"I thought faeries were gentler than elves. But you are far lovelier," Kiera observed with a long breath out.

This made the queen giggle more.

"Well, thank you. But that wasn't really a question," she pointed out, walking down the white corridor.

"Sorry. I um, I just thought you were the queen on your own. So, are you the ruler or is he?"

"We both are," the queen replied, stifling more giggles.

"Both equally?"

"Yes."

"Wow, OK. I mean, that's really nice."

"I think you had better have some tea, sweet girl. It will help calm you and then we can have lots of fun. You can ask as many questions as you like. I'm sure you're bursting with hundreds of them."

They entered a reception room. It was a lot smaller than Kiera had expected. It felt warm and homely despite the amount of white. It felt softer and more welcoming than the one Queen Una had shown them to in the faery's domain.

Sitting in a large white chair was a magnificent male elf. He stood as soon as the doors opened, admitting the ladies into his presence. He bowed smartly. Kiera and Frydah dipped into curtseys.

"Ah, there you are. It is a delight to make your acquaintance," he announced.

Nora was welcomed into his outstretched arms and received a peck on her cheek.

Kiera saw and felt the love between the royal couple. It was beautiful, yet made her suddenly sad. A thought was trying to cloud her happiness, but she couldn't quite make out what it was. The queen was immediately aware of her guest's uneasiness and guided her to one of the many chairs.

"Perhaps you are weary after your journey?" she enquired.

"Oh no. I'm full of beans. I feel alive with energy."

A servant had poured them each a cup of golden coloured tea, and set the cups on tables near each person.

"Try this, it cures all which ails you," the king offered in his smooth, rich voice.

Kiera held the delicate cup to her lips, and quickly checked for anything untoward which may have been snuck into her drink. Happy she wasn't being drugged yet again, she sipped and moaned in appreciation. This tea was slightly spicy and of course very sweet.

"Delicious," she declared.

"Ah, that's much better. I was concerned for a moment. But now I see you smiling once more I am satisfied," the king noted.

Kiera couldn't help but stare at him. His hair was long and black, but his eyes were golden. He was impressive, handsome and imposing all at once.

Noticing her observation of him, he glared straight into Kiera's eyes. She felt intimidated but refused to look away. He was actually the one to look away first, and he chuckled as he did so.

"Haha, you're a strong, brave girl. You'll be just fine, Kiera," he told her.

Kiera wasn't quite sure what to say in response and just blushed, turning her gaze towards the white floor.

After a moment, she found the courage to look up and ask, "Pardon me, but what is your name?"

"Oh yes, our introductions were interrupted. My apologies. My name is Alfred."

"Nora tells me you rule together here."

"Yes, she speaks true."

"You do not seem very alike."

"I am the yin to her yang, you might say. She is all sweetness, and I am rather gruffer. But you have nothing to fear from me, I swear it."

"Do the elves require much leadership?" she asked, turning to Nora, who was easier to converse with.

"Not really. We do not need to rule with an iron fist. We are here to maintain the tranquillity. We oversee life here."

"Queen Una is the ruler of the faeries, but I think she is also the overseer of the fae realm?"

"Yes, we answer to her ultimately, but she does not tend to interfere. The fae realm is a happy land generally."

"She told me the daoi-sith tried to follow me here but was not allowed entry."

"Did he? Oh dear me. He must be desperate to reach you indeed. No, he would not be able to enter this realm. Only those who contain more light than darkness are permitted. It was not always so, and there were dark times."

"Were all dark entities forced into the human realm then?"

"Oh, such a miserable topic. I know I said I'd answer your questions, but I was hoping you would have a happier theme."

"I am sorry, Queen Nora. You are right," Kiera replied, biting her lip.

"I did not mean to be evasive. However, I do have a question for you."

"For me?"

"Yes. Are you bored of dancing yet?"

"No, I don't think I could ever tire of that."

"Oh good. We are holding a ball this evening in your honour, but I did not want to force you if you did not wish it. Our balls are not quite as…lively as the faery dance. "

"In my honour? I think my head will start to swell if I have any more honours bestowed upon me."

"Kiera, you are very special. We have heard of your peace making with the elinefae. And you apparently have incredible healing powers. You are unique, a beautiful blend of elinefae and sorceress. Your light quotient is one of the highest I've ever seen."

"I'm just me."

"And that is what makes you so adorable. You are grounded and honest. Such goodness must be protected."

"Protected? Am I in danger?"

"Not here. But there is a lot of darkness in your realm. I would hate to see anything happen to you."

"Err, that's kind of you," Kiera said, grimacing, not sure whether to take that as a threat or not.

"Oh dear, I made you frown again. You are quite safe here."

"Sorry. I'm a little overwhelmed."

"Of course. We all must seem very strange to one who's been brought up by humans. You poor dear. I can't imagine how much of a shock you've had. Why don't you go with your faery guide to one of the guest rooms, and we'll send someone to dress you."

Kiera cocked her head to one side and scrunched her nose.

"A dress for the ball," Nora clarified.

"Oh, yeah, sure. Thank you."

Kiera and Frydah were led away.

"Well, what do you make of her?" Nora asked her husband.

"She's like a frightened butterfly."

Chapter 25 – Elf Balls

Both Kiera and Frydah were measured by a seamstress, who instantly conjured up marvellous ball gowns for them. Frydah's was a strapless gold dress; sparklier on the top with long, flowing, swishing golden skirts with trails of sparkles interspersed. The colour matched her wings beautifully, which she fluttered as she admired her reflection.

Kiera's ball gown was forest green velvet, and more medieval in style. The neckline plunged deeply into a creamy gold section which ran down the centre of her body, all the way to the floor. Tiny green ivy leaves were embroidered on the fabric. The sleeves hung below the back of her hands.

Kiera was amazed how each dress was matched them perfectly, and yet displayed the colours of the court. And all prepared within moments. She joined Frydah at the mirror and gazed at the princess she saw there.

Her circlet was sitting on her long loose brown curls. Her makeup was natural yet shimmered in the light. Touching her face, she checked it really was her own reflection she was looking at.

The dressmaker had left as soon as she was happy her work was complete. The girls were alone.

"I could get used to this," Kiera admitted with a wry smile.

"Don't get too used to it," Frydah warned good-naturedly.

"It's just so wonderful here. I feel so light and happy. But something's wrong. I feel at odds with everyone I meet. I'm not quite sure who to trust, except Colle of course."

"That's because you can never fully trust fae. Their darkness may be kept in check, but many are still quite manipulative. Especially when they're trying to win over a mighty protector."

"Is that what I am? They see me as a protector?"

"Kiera, darling, you are many fine things. Protector is one of them. Keeper of the peace, healer, all round lovely girl."

"Oh stop, you'll make me blush," she chuckled, giving Frydah a playful push.

"Why else would we be getting the royal treatment?"

"But they already have a safe place."

"There's never any harm in adding to your safety."

"So do I need to choose one type of fae to protect?"

Frydah snapped her fingers and clapped her hands in front of Kiera's face.

"Oi, stupid. We're not staying here, so no," she reminded her.

Frydah began to worry they'd stayed too long already. The fae realm was mesmerising. It was so alluring that one could easily be convinced to remain indefinitely.

She wondered if that was the reason Queen Una had seemed so odd; perhaps she was trying to lure Kiera into doing just that? Her thoughts were interrupted by a knock at the door. A valet entered, carrying a tray of drinks.

"Thank you," Kiera acknowledged, "Will we be here long?"

"Not too long, ma'am. The king and queen are preparing. They wish to ensure everyone is gathered for your entrance," he informed her with a nod of his head.

"Thank you. I'm sorry, I don't know your name."

"My name? Well, it's Roarke, ma'am," he stuttered.

"Thank you, Roarke. Will you come back when it's time for us to go?"

"If you like, ma'am," he replied as he bowed and backed towards the door.

Kiera smiled at the shy servant as he closed the door.

"Oh that's sad. Why should he be surprised at me asking his name? Are elves so insensitive to others? I must say I'm disappointed. I thought they'd be better than humans."

Frydah kissed her friend's cheek and told her, "And that's why you're so lovely."

"Because I asked a being their name?"

"Because you care about everyone, and you try to see the best in them all."

They hugged briefly before Kiera's curiosity got the better of her, and she crossed over to the tray. There were three jugs of clear liquid, which she sniffed.

"I'm guessing none of these are plain water?"

"No, let's see. This will be fuchsia flavoured, this one poppy and this is, ooh cherry blossom," she said grabbing the last jug and pouring herself a drink.

Kiera had swept the drinks on her approach, ensuring these too were safe. She opted for the same as Frydah and took a sip.

"Mm, most refreshing," she approved, taking a big slurp.

"Everything will taste so bland when we get back to your home," Frydah commented with a hint of sadness.

They quickly finished their drinks and sat down, waiting to be summonsed.

"Elf balls are quite formal. They're very different from the fun faery dances."

"Will I be expected to dance?"

"Oh yes."

"But I don't know how."

"You do. You just don't know you do. It's OK. Your feet will magickally lead you. Just don't fight them, otherwise you'll fall over."

"How reassuring," Kiera mused, raising an eyebrow.

"Just go with the flow. You'll be fine."

"Go with the flow," she repeated on a long breath, trying to calm her building nerves.

Kiera jumped when Roarke knocked at their door again. Her hand was on her chest, trying to still her fluttering heart as he entered.

"They are ready now, ma'am," he announced with a smile.

"Thank you, Roarke," she said shakily as she stood on slightly wobbly legs.

She bit her lip as she crossed the room, Frydah at her side. As she passed the valet, he touched her hand.

"You'll be fine," he whispered kindly before leading the way down the maze of corridors.

As the large gold doors were opened, Kiera found herself at the top of a beautiful white staircase lined with gold carpet, gazing over a sea of elves. Her breath caught in her chest. This was so much more than she'd been expecting.

"Elinefae Sorceress Kiera and Faery Frydah," someone announced loudly by their side.

Any eyes which hadn't been on them already now turned in their direction. Kiera could hear gasps and whispers. She prayed not to fall whilst descending the staircase, and was grateful to have Frydah by her side. She felt like a freaky spectacle again.

A path opened up, leading the pair to the dais at the far end of the room where the king and queen stood in front of two ornately decorated gold thrones. Queen Nora stretched her arms out as Kiera approached, and welcomed her warmly.

At the queen's signal, the band began to play, and the dancing began. Kiera and Frydah were directed to chairs just to the side of the thrones, so they could observe and be observed.

Queen Nora was wearing a large white ball gown, with white lace across her chest and down her arms, all highlighted with gold accents. She was dancing with King Alfred, who was dressed all in black with gold embroidery. They led the first dance together.

Kiera winced as the chattering grew louder, but relaxed as the sound was muffled, as if someone had placed cotton wool in her ears. She glanced over at Frydah who smiled at her.

'*Many thanks,*' Kiera told her friend telepathically.

Frydah dipped her head subtly and turned her attention back to the room. Kiera took deep breaths, trying to steady her nerves.

Kiera had time to take in her surroundings. The great hall was white and gold, and she began to think the obsession with those colours was getting a bit much.

Servants lined the walls, ready for any request made by the numerous elves present. The guests were dressed in an array of colours, which gladdened Kiera's heart. It was nice to see colours again. They all looked incredibly elegant as they waltzed around the room. The swaying movement was hypnotic.

After just one dance, the king and queen returned to the dais, but with two young males following them. They were offered as dance partners to Kiera and Frydah, who were unable to refuse, despite how much Kiera wanted to remain seated.

The girls were led onto the dancefloor, with Kiera biting her lip. But her nerves flew away as soon as the music started, and she was held in strong male hands. She had to admit her dance partner was quite good looking.

He swept her around in circles. Kiera found her feet gliding across the floor. She remembered Frydah's instruction to go with the flow, and that's just what she did. Music filled her entire being, and she allowed it to take control of her, completely abandoning herself to the dance.

As the music ended, her dance partner bowed low and told her, "You dance beautifully. Thank you for the honour of the dance. I will never forget it. It is a memory I will treasure for the rest of my days."

Kiera smiled bashfully, but found another elf was taking his place already.

"May I have the honour of the next dance?" he formally asked her.

Kiera willingly accepted the invitation, and found herself skipping along to a sort of polka. The people around her blurred as she span around the room with the male who was leading. A stone plummeted in her stomach as she wished Pryderi was here instead of him.

Pryderi; she'd almost forgotten about him. How could she? Guilt flooded her system, but she tried to plaster a smile on her face, not wanting to appear rude to her hosts. They seemed to want her to only feel happiness, and had gone to great lengths for her benefit.

Another male took her current partner's place, and Kiera skipped down the room in a quickstep. Kiera had seen similar dances before, but as Frydah had said, had been unaware she could actually dance like that herself.

She tried really hard to abandon herself to the music, but was unable to fully commit. Pryderi was seeping into her consciousness. Her smile began to fade.

'Are you alright?' Frydah asked in her head.

'Of course,' Kiera smiled, trying harder to push her gloomy thoughts away.

Another melody and another partner took Kiera off into a foxtrot. She walked smoothly with long strides across the ballroom, rising and falling gracefully. And took shorter steps on tiptoe when guided to by her own feet, followed by slower ones on her heels.

Although her body was following the dance steps her mind was travelling far away. As she tried to push him further away, Pryderi was only becoming stronger in her mind.

By the time the dance ended, the thought had become deafening. Kiera slapped her hands over her ears, and gazed around the room, feeling dizzy. Faster and faster it span, until she collapsed onto the floor, clutching her head. Frydah was by her side in an instant.

"Kiera, Kiera, what's wrong?" the faery was asking in a panicked tone.

"Alright, give them some room," a male was ushering people away from the two girls.

Frydah looked up only to discover it was Roarke. He bent down next to them.

"May I?" he asked Frydah, who nodded eagerly.

He picked Kiera up in his strong arms and swiftly carried her out of the ballroom, and into the nearest empty room he could find. He laid her down on a chaise longue. She'd remained curled up and crying in his arms all the way.

"Pryderi," she screamed.

"Oh my goddess. Pryderi? Is something wrong?"

"Yes. I need him. He needs me. I must go to him," Kiera said between sobs.

The pain had spread through her whole body.

"Wait!" Frydah just about managed to stop her friend transporting herself away.

"Wait. We will go to him, I promise. But we will go to Cerys first. You will be too weak to help immediately. Will you let me help you?"

"Yes, just hurry, please," she wailed.

"Thank you for your assistance. And please apologise for us," she said, dismissing Roarke who had been looking on anxiously.

"Of course. Is there anything further I can do?"

"Thank you, but no. Not for now. We must go."

With that, Frydah held Kiera's hand, changed their outfits back to normal and transported them to the spare room in Cerys' cottage.

Chapter 26 – Help

Unfortunately, the spare room was occupied. The girls bumped into Threaris as they arrived. Her father caught Kiera as she stumbled.

"Oh my goddess, are you OK?" he asked, concern etched on his face.

He guided her to the bed so she could sit, but she laid down, overwhelmed by the wave of dizziness and nausea that assaulted her upon her entrance back into the human realm.

"We need smelling salts," Frydah instructed the sorcerer, who immediately rushed off to find some.

Hearing the commotion, Zondra rushed into the room.

"Oh goodness," she muttered upon seeing the sorry scene.

She began to sing softly, which immediately started to soothe Kiera. She rolled over onto her back, her forearm resting on her forehead.

Threaris returned and wafted the smelling salts under his daughter's nose, making it wrinkle in disgust.

"Eurgh," she muttered, scrunching her eyes too.

Ignoring her protests, Threaris passed the smelling salts by her again. This time she managed to sit up, pushing his arm away.

"That's enough of those, thank you," she said groggily.

"What on Earth happened? She was supposed to be with the fae so she'd be safe," he gruffed.

"She was, but something's wrong with Pryderi. It must be very bad for her to feel it all the way there."

"He was feeling unwell, I believe. Cerys and Chen are with him now."

"See, he is being looked after."

"I must go to him," Kiera insisted through her still foggy mind.

"Just as soon as you're up to it we shall."

"Err, alas I am unable to accompany you," Threaris apologised.

"Are you still hiding from Rhion?"

"Well yes, but that is not why. I am incognito at present. Whilst I remain here Donnagan cannot see me."

"Oh, so you are hiding from the dark elf?"

"Yes, but only because I need to keep the element of surprise. He thinks I'm dead, you see."

"And why would he think that?"

"Because he believes he killed me."

"What?" Kiera was fully alert now.

Zondra's song stopped.

"Oh it's nothing really. Just a little scuffle which went a little wrong. Zondra saved me. I'm fine."

"You fought with him?"

"It's a long story, and you seem a lot better. Should you not be hurrying to Pryderi?"

Kiera scowled at the sorcerer.

"Yes, but I will be asking you for more details as soon as I'm back."

"Very well."

Kiera grabbed Frydah's hand, preparing to go to where she so desperately needed to be.

"Are you coming?" Kiera asked Zondra.

She sidled up to Threaris, who wrapped his arm around her shoulders.

"My place is here for now," she told Kiera.

Looking at the pair, Kiera absorbed their appearance as a couple in stunned silence. But there was no time for that now. She transported herself and Frydah to Pryderi's room.

"Kiera," he was wailing from his cot, clutching his stomach.

"I'm here," she told him, rushing past Cerys, kneeling at his side.

She brushed his hair, trying to soothe him, but in that moment the full force of their separation hit her. Whilst in the fae realm she'd been separated from that pain.

Upon her return she'd felt only dizziness and disorientation. Zondra's song had soothed her. In the fae realm she'd been cocooned in peace and happiness, wrapped up from any hurt. But now it crushed her.

Folding up in her own pain, she managed to grasp onto Pryderi's hand. He squeezed back. Both of them were clinging on like a drowning man to a rock.

"Oh for the love of the goddess," Cerys muttered.

Chen grabbed another flannel and drenched that in the warm herbed water he'd already prepared for Pryderi. He passed it to Cerys who held it to Kiera's head.

"You're together now. There there,"

Looking at Chen she asked, "Will you help me lift her up? Maybe they'll feel better if they're lying together."

Chen didn't hesitate. He lifted Kiera up onto the cot, and settled her next to her mate. They instantly wrapped their arms around one another, sobbing.

"You were gone so far away. I could barely feel you. It hurt," Pryderi cried into her neck.

"I'm sorry. I had to go. I wasn't safe," she wept back.

"I know. But you were away so long,"

"I was only gone a couple of days."

"Weeks," he corrected.

"Weeks?" she asked, her eyes going wide.

Kiera was sure it had only been a matter of days. How could it have been so long? Right now she didn't care, and held Pryderi as tightly as possible.

His lips softly brushed hers before deepening his kiss. Her mouth opened to him, welcoming his attention. Their hands began to wander as their passion increased.

"Aher, I think that's our cue to leave," Cerys said to Chen, clearing her throat.

The witches crept out of the room, closing the door behind them. Frydah joined them. Cerys set a sound barrier up, thinking Kiera was too preoccupied to do so herself. They stood guard, ensuring the pair had privacy whilst they healed each other.

"Stand guard, I'll fetch them something to eat," Cerys told Chen.

Away she scurried. Chen stood like a security officer, which he supposed he now was. He realised nobody must know Kiera was here. But he also recognised the necessity of her presence.

"How long has he been like this?" Frydah asked.

"He's been gradually getting worse over the weeks. We have been called to aid him often. But as time wore on there was less and less we could do to ease his suffering. When two soul matched people are torn asunder it is only a matter of time until they wither away and die."

"I had not expected this. I should have thought. Sorry," Frydah said, her wings drooping.

"I am just relieved Kiera is here. But nobody must discover her. Rhion is as stubborn as ever in his denial of the relationship. He refuses to see the torment his Watcher has been enduring."

"There is something unnatural here."

Frydah popped out of view as footsteps sounded.

Elan prowled along the corridor. Chen stiffened his stance, making sure he was blocking the doorway.

"What is this? You would deny me entry?" Elan asked with a scowl.

"He is resting, Elan. He must not be disturbed," Chen said calmly yet firmly.

"But I am his friend."

"I am sorry. He has been gravely ill and needs his rest. I must ask that you come back later."

Cerys returned just then and was carrying a plate of venison and a glass of blood.

"He requires all that?" Elan asked her.

"Yes, he will when he wakes," she told him, backing up the cover story Chen had just thought at her.

"Then he really is that ill?"

"He has been. We've been healing him, and hopefully this will restore him."

"I cannot understand why our Leader would let it get this far," Elan commented, shaking his head sadly.

"Pryderi will need your help. You and Arwyn must keep an eye on him."

"We always have."

"I know. I did not mean to cause insult. You know what I mean. Extra care. This is a great strain for him."

"You have my word," he said, lowering his head and clutching his fist to his heart centre.

"Thank you. Would you like me to alert you when he is up to visitors?"

"For this I would be grateful. I am off to my rest, but please do wake me as soon as I can see him."

"Of course."

Elan accepted the witch's advice, but his lip still curled as he stalked towards his den.

'Phew, that was too close,' Cerys quietly observed.

'I did not think he would go. I thought I would have to fight that stubborn elinefae.'

'You would have handled him.'

'Maybe, but I do not welcome any fight.'

'I know. It's part of the reason I love you.'

Chen took the plate and glass from her hand, and placed it on the floor. He stepped in close and stole a kiss in this quiet moment together.

Cerys pulled away before things became too heated. They had a job to do after all. She quickly checked to see if there were any noises behind her shield, and heard muffled voices.

Straightening her skirts and hair, she knocked on the door before entering with her edible offerings.

The pair were lying in bed together but were too happy together to mind Cerys' interruption.

"I brought you these," she told them in her sing-song voice.

"Thank you," Kiera said to the witch's retreating back.

"Just make sure you don't linger long. Elan's already tried to see your mate, and was upset at being turned away," she informed them, looking over her shoulder.

"I shall make amends later. Thank you," Pryderi added in his even deeper, post-coital tone.

Cerys quickly shut the door behind her as she re-joined Chen on guard duty.

'Are they OK?'

'A picture of health.'

Back inside the room, the mated pair were tackling their meal with gusto. Kiera, having only just returned from the fae realm was ravenous, especially after her activity with Pryderi. He let her drink the glass of blood, acknowledging her need was greater. He'd find his own later if he required it.

They both felt so much happier and healthier, but as the energy of the food coursed through them, reality started to sink in. Cerys' words of warning echoed in their hearts and minds.

"I wish I didn't have to go," Kiera said sadly, stroking the back of her mate's head.

"I do not know how much longer I can do this. I cannot bear our parting," he told her, pawing her cheek.

"I miss you so much," she confessed, tears already threatening.

"I love you, Kiera."

"I love you too. We must be patient. Just a little longer. I will speak with my father. He fought Donnagan. Maybe we can unite and try again."

"No, I will not see you in harm's way," he told her fiercely.

"I will not do anything stupid."

"Kiera, I cannot and will not lose you."

"You won't."

"Please, do not do this."

"I may have to. Do not make me pledge a promise I cannot keep."

"Promise you will call me to you if you do fight. I need to be there. I will feel your danger. It will drive me mad if I am not by your side."

"I promise," she vowed, looking straight into his eyes.

They drew their foreheads together, taking deep breaths, desperate to feel their closeness before their imminent separation.

"I must go." Kiera sighed.

"I know."

Not being able to face a lengthy goodbye Kiera transported herself back to Cerys' cottage, Frydah following in her wake.

Pryderi was left with cold, empty arms again. He sat up, gripping tightly to the edge of his cot. It took him several minutes to compose himself. But finally, with a grunt, he brought himself to his feet.

He paced around his room, trying to cling onto the feeling of unity, reaching out across their link, testing Kiera's close proximity. She was at least a lot closer now. She'd been so far away in the fae realm he'd barely been able to sense her at all. It had been excruciating.

Continuing to breathe deeply, he strode across the room and opened the door to the witches.

Chapter 27 – Purpose

"I need to go and check on Kiera," Cerys announced as she walked into the room.

"Fine. I will remain here," Chen said.

"But I am much better now," Pryderi tried to tell them.

"Yes, but you are not supposed to be," Chen reminded him.

"Oh, of course." He collapsed back down on the bed, his hands covering his face.

Cerys rubbed the elinefae's arm. "I will check what we can do. Threaris was scheming, but with Kiera's return, perhaps she will spur him on. I believe he is hesitating because of his previous failure. Bloody man."

With that, Cerys travelled to her own home via the portal. Threaris was fussing over Kiera, making sure she was as recovered as she said she was. Zondra stood smiling at the pair.

"It is nice to see them as father and daughter, is it not?" Zondra addressed Cerys.

"Indeed it is. Far more pleasant. But I fear we really should not delay. Now she's back here, it will not take Donnagan long to notice and act. We must be ready. Her mate does not wish her to fight though."

"He's not the only one," Frydah added.

"Who else is against it?" Zondra enquired.

"Queen Una herself, it seems. Not that she said as much, of course. But intelligence insinuates this to be the case."

"How curious. I don't know why she should be so concerned," Cerys grumbled.

"We were trying to find out from the elves when Kiera collapsed and we had to return here."

"You were with the elves?"

"Oh yes. Queen Nora and King Alfred were throwing a marvellous ball for her."

"Well, I'm pleased you were having a jolly time," Cerys said in a tone which suggested quite the opposite.

"We had a wonderful time, and everybody loved Kiera. There was much dancing and celebrating in her name. She's something of a celebrity," Frydah said, clapping her hands.

Threaris couldn't hide his smile. He was proud of his daughter, and it showed.

"And you're pleased with this?" Cerys grumbled at Threaris.

"Why should I not be?"

"Is it not curious that she is held in such high esteem?"

"Are you saying my daughter is unworthy of such attention?"

"Of course not. She's a lovely girl. But it sounds as if she was worshipped more like a deity."

"And you're worried she'll get a swollen head?"

"No, I'm concerned others have an ulterior motive behind such public displays."

"Cerys, they are fae. Showing their happiness and dancing is just what they do."

"Hello, *she* is right here," Kiera finally managed to get a word in edgewise, waving at them.

"Of course you are, dear. Sorry. It's just we're concerned."

"Maybe if we concentrated on eradicating an evil elf there'd be slightly less reason to be worried?"

"Well, you have a point there," Cerys agreed.

"Great. So what are we going to do?"

"There is no we, Kiera. I may have different motivation, but you are not to face him," Threaris told her.

"You need all the help you can get from what I gather. Zondra had to rescue you last time you faced Donnagan. All those fae recognised my power. Maybe you should too."

Threaris looked a little downcast by her outburst.

Taking a deep breath, he told her, "I do recognise your power. I just don't want to put you in harm's way."

"Funny you didn't think of that when you were going to kill me so you could escape."

"Kiera! Where did that come from? That was not your father. That was the daoi-sith, not Threaris, and you know it. That was not fair," Frydah challenged.

Kiera clapped her hand over her mouth. "I'm so sorry. I didn't mean that. I don't know why I said it."

Worried glances passed around the room.

"He cannot get through this barrier, can he? Your tether was left where you fell," Zondra thought out loud.

"He shouldn't be able to, and yes, I left the tether behind. You saw me."

"But that was definitely not our Kiera."

"You are correct," he said, approaching Kiera and checking her eyes, turning her head to the light so he could see more clearly.

Kiera shook herself away from his grasp.

"Can I be angry in my own right?"

"Yes, but only about things which you mean. You said yourself you didn't mean it. So, where did it come from?"

Kiera plonked down into a sofa as she sighed, "I don't know. I'm just confused and tired and hungry."

"She has only just returned from the fae realm," Frydah suggested, "Hmm, well how about we try to ensure you're fed and rested? We can discuss plans of action later."

"And treating me like a child helps how?"

"And there it goes again," Threaris noted with a wry smile.

"I'm still going with the hangry theory," Frydah told him.

"I hope you're right."

"She's more protected than Queen Una surrounded by a herd of unicorns. And look at her eyes. They're dull."

Kiera ignored them all, walked out into the garden, and bent down to the pond.

Shui took flight with a whoosh. He'd grown just large enough for his mission. Kiera sat outside as she waited, sniffing in the petrichor of the falling rain. Despite the moisture landing on her skin, she was enjoying the moment. It felt good to enjoy the fresh air again.

Everything in the fae realm had smelled sweet, which was lovely. But nothing could beat the fresh scent now pervading her nostrils.

Gazing into the pond, she looked at her reflection, which was fractured by falling raindrops.

It didn't take Shui long to return. Kiera hadn't liked asking him to run an errand for her, but didn't want to cross the boundary herself. She'd promised Pryderi not to do anything foolish.

Shui hovered and dropped a bloody deer carcass at her feet before landing with a thump next to her.

"Thank you, my friend."

She offered him first bite for his trouble, which he readily accepted. He left Kiera the lion's share though, which she devoured greedily, her lips smacking loudly. The subsistence she'd consumed with Pryderi had only acted as an appetiser.

The others had remained inside the cottage where it was warm and dry. They were looking through the window, curious at first what Kiera was up to, and were relieved when they witnessed her feeding.

Threaris clothed himself in a long raincoat, and grabbed an umbrella from the stand by the door.

"Feeling better?" he asked his daughter who was still crouching on the ground.

She leaped to her feet. "Much, thank you."

Her grin was lined by bright red blood, making Threaris wince.

"What?" she shrugged.

He pointed at his own mouth whilst informing her, "You have a little something here."

She wiped her mouth with her arm, making her father wince more.

"Oh really. Manners, please."

Rain was drumming on the canopy of his umbrella.

"You're quite right," she admitted, and whistled at Shui.

The dragon lolloped over and crunched down the animal bones.

Threaris shuddered. "That's not what I meant and you know it. Are you ready to join us yet?"

Kiera magicked away the lingering traces of blood, and followed her father inside. Once back in the dry, and out of his wet things, Threaris checked Kiera's eyes again.

"Well, your eyes are brighter. I suppose the faery was correct."

"The faery has a name, and you should not sound so surprised," Frydah said, hovering with her hands on her hips, and wearing her best scowl.

"My apologies. You have the right of it, Frydah. Cerys might I trouble you for a mint, please?"

Cerys went to a drawer and pulled out a tube of mints, smirking. She knew how sensitive he was to the sight of blood. Even Donnagan had not been able to stop the sorcerer's vegetarianism. She'd been surprised he'd ventured outside, and not just waited for Kiera to come back in. But she was comforted that this must mean he had a very great and genuine concern for his daughter.

"What are you all staring at?" Kiera asked.

"Nothing, nothing," Frydah deflected.

"Good. Are we all fed and happy?"

"Yes," they all chimed.

"Good. Because we have a dark elf to catch."

"You have a plan?" Zondra asked.

"You bet, and it's a good one."

Chapter 28 – A Dark Hunt

Kiera divulged her plan which had been inspired by her quiet contemplation outside.

"Very well," Threaris reluctantly agreed, "But for now we need rest. We should attack tomorrow at dusk as the shadows fall and he believes he has the advantage."

The others approved. Threaris and Zondra walked towards the spare room.

Frydah scrunched up her nose. "And where are you to sleep?"

"I'm not sleepy anyway."

"Oh, that sofa pulls out into a bed," Cerys informed her, pointing at said sofa.

"There's bedding in that box over there if you need it," she added, motioning towards a trunk in the corner of the room.

Cerys made her way quietly upstairs with butterflies in her tummy. She had agreed to Kiera's plan as it seemed sensible, but it was not without its dangers. Concern furrowed her brow.

Sitting at her dresser, she called Chen, using the mirror. "How's the patient?"

"Better than he should be."

"Can you come home without rousing suspicion?"

"Yes. Are you alright?"

"Fine. I just need you here quickly."

"OK, I'll call Shui."

He got off the call, and immediately called for his companion, who landed in a quiet spot of the clan's land. Chen jogged over to him, and away they flew into the night, through the wind and the rain.

His arrival made Kiera jump as he walked through the door. With a quick apology and greeting, he ran upstairs to join Cerys. She was already snuggled under the covers of her bed. Stripping, he settled in next to her.

Stroking her hair aside, kissing behind her ear, he whispered, "Now will you tell me what is wrong?"

"We attack tomorrow."

"Oh. I feel we have been waiting a long time, but yet it is happening suddenly."

"I knew Kiera's impatience would speed things along, but not this fast. Her very impatience troubles me."

"You think she leaps in without thought?"

"I think she is too eager for what she does not yet understand."

"But Threaris would not let her do anything rash."

"Has he not already proved his own impulsiveness? It is the sorcerer's way, I suppose."

"Tell me what you need me to do."

She went over the plans as she nestled in his strong, reassuring arms.

***

Kiera was sitting on the sofa bed, which Frydah had insisted on her pulling out in case she could rest. Kiera's knees were pulled up to her chest with her arms wrapped around them, and her head resting on top, chewing her lip.

"You are worried," Frydah observed.

"Yes, how can I not be? My father thought he could take on the daoi-sith, and it almost cost him his life."

"But you are not alone. Two sorcerers are better than one."

"Are you alright doing your faery thing? Do you need help?"

"Well, I would always be happy for more hands. Did you have someone in mind?"

"Well, I was thinking maybe Colle. He is very wise, and I instinctively trust him."

"I'll contact him and ask. I cannot demand," she said, starting to take flight so she could make the call in private.

"Frydah," Kiera called, stopping her from flying off.

"Yes?"

"Why is he so chubby? I don't mean to be rude, but most faeries are skinny little beings."

"Oh, that's because he soaks up more magick than the rest of us. He's been around a very long time, and seems to have extra capacity." Frydah giggled.

"Does magick make you fat?" Kiera asked, perplexed.

"Not normally. I think he's just a bit greedy."

"But it hasn't made him arrogant or controlling."

Frydah rolled her eyes as she reminded her friend, "Kiera, he's a faery."

"Yeah, but he's good. It's not like that sorceress we met at my father's. She was really snooty, like she ruled the world."

"That is just personality. There is no good magick or bad magick, just the person who wields it. Have you not worked that one out yet?"

Kiera was left pondering that thought as Frydah disappeared to contact Colle. She contacted Pryderi to tell him he had to feign illness the next day still, so he didn't go on patrol. She instructed him to rest until she contacted him late afternoon. Not daring to risk giving him details, she told him just enough so he knew the attack was imminent.

***

Zondra and Threaris were secluded in the spare room, sitting next to each other on the bed. Threaris kept getting up and pacing before sitting back down.

"I don't like my daughter putting herself in danger."

"But we will all be there. We will protect her," Zondra reassured him.

"I thought I was protected and look what happened to me."

"I was there to save you."

"Only because he wasn't aware of your presence."

"As he won't be aware of yours, or any of us, until it's too late."

"I still don't like it."

"You have to have faith. Trust in Kiera, her abilities, and us."

"I do. I just don't trust him."

"And it is wise not to. But we have to do this."

"Yes we must, but I still don't have to like it."

They discussed their roles in detail. Threaris kept pacing long into the night.

***

Nobody seemed to get much rest that night. There was too much to think about and too many worries buzzed around their heads.

They all convened early the next morning, coffee in hand to help clear their muzzy minds. They spent the day discussing their plans further.

Chen had to go to the clan to attend to Pryderi, to keep up the pretence of his ill health. He took the opportunity to fill him in on the details of what was to happen that evening.

Cerys made lunch, but nobody was able to eat much. They tried to rest to gather energy, but that didn't work either. You could cut the tension with a knife.

Threaris almost wore a hole in the carpet with his pacing until Zondra sang at him. He was at least able to sit as a result, but his knee kept jigging up and down.

Time drew on agonisingly slowly, but at last, the hour approached. Colle appeared promptly, and Frydah went through what was expected of him.

Kiera called Pryderi and Chen to her, transporting them to the cottage. They'd been ensconced in Pryderi's den all day. Elan had been in to check on him as his only visitor. Nobody should feel the need to see him until the next shift change, and Kiera hoped to get him back home by then.

Stealing a moment, she hugged and kissed Pryderi, reassuring herself as much as him that they were going to be alright.

They were as battle ready as they'd ever be. Forming a circle, they offered prayers to the goddess to watch over them.

Frydah and Kiera transported everyone to the battle's location. They'd tracked the dark elf down. His energy signature after the battle had suggested he'd been injured in his fight with the sorcerer, and he'd gone to ground in the only home he'd known for many years; the cave in the cliffs adjacent to the sorcerer's former home.

Donnagan had managed to heal since his battle, but Kiera sensed he'd not regained full health. Something was wrong. That is why she'd been keen to attack now, before he was at maximum strength. They needed their enemy to be as weak as possible.

There wasn't much cover to be had since the house was no longer standing, but there was a small glade near Donnagan's cave. The faeries hid between the rocks of the outcrop. Zondra perched on a ledge below the cliff's edge.

Threaris, Pryderi and the witches hid behind the trees. Shui had flown to them, and shrunk down as small as possible, latching onto the cliff next to the trees.

Kiera stood at the entrance of the glade, seemingly alone. She placed a veil of invisibility behind her, hiding her companions. The energy would have her signature only, so Donnagan wouldn't suspect anyone else was there.

Appearing inside Donnagan's cave, deep in the cliff, she saw him clearly through the gloom.

"You have been looking for me," she stated imperiously.

The daoi-sith leapt at her sudden appearance. "Yes. How did you find me?"

"It wasn't difficult. It was the first place I looked. Not exactly subtle are you?"

His shock had worn off, and his confidence was growing. She was in his lair. This was his territory and the last of Threaris' line was standing in front of him, just where he needed her to be. She would not survive long.

"Why should I hide? I am not afraid of you. It is for you to fear me," he told her in a tone oozing with superiority.

"You are sure you should not fear me?" she asked with an amused raise of her eyebrow.

Donnagan had begun to slowly edge around, he was clearly trying to get behind Kiera to block her exit.

"I'm sure. Your father showed the same arrogance, and so I killed him," he said with an evil gleam.

"You show pride at taking the life of another?"

"I enjoyed killing him. All those years living in his shadow, it was sickening. But finally thanks to you I was able to end his miserable life."

"A life you made miserable."

"No, I made him glorious."

"By killing all those elinefae?"

"Yes, those bastards deserved to die. And his name echoed across the lands in tribute."

"Tribute? This is what you call it? You show no remorse at all? You do not regret killing all those innocent people?"

"Nobody is ever innocent, foolish girl."

"Funny, I didn't believe anyone was truly evil. Our beliefs can be changed it seems."

"You call me evil? What about them?"

"My father gave you a chance. You think killing him was right?"

"A chance? He and those cats killed my kind. Was that not evil?"

"Your kind were inflicting pain and misery wherever you went. Darkness was diminishing light. You needed to be stopped."

"Enough of this," he snapped, jumping in front of the entrance.

"So you will kill me? And not accept help?"

"You're the one who needs help," he declared as he stretched out his arm.

Purple sparks flew from his fingers and a bolt of purple energy flew towards her. Kiera disappeared. The purple bolt bounced off the cave wall and hit the floor.

Grunting in frustration, Donnagan tried to feel around him for her energy signature. Where had she gone? She shouldn't have been able to summon her own magick here.

"If you want me you'll have to try harder than that," her voice echoed down the cave's tunnel to him.

In a rage, he rushed towards the sound of her voice.

"You think you are safe outside? Only a fool would attack a daoi-sith in the hour of shadows."

Running outside, he saw her standing at the edge of the glade, where she'd been standing the whole time. She had merely projected an image of herself into the cave. She'd got the idea when she saw her reflection in Shui's pond.

"Oh, you're just making it too easy. That's not fun. At least don't stand quite so near the shadows," he sneered.

Kiera's necklace felt cool against her skin, and her ring glowed bright white as a purple energy bolt shot from Donnagan's hand.

Several things happened at once. Threaris rushed forwards, shooting a blue bolt to intercede the daoi-sith's purple one. Pryderi ran and flung himself in front of Kiera. Frydah flung golden sparks in front of her friend. And Shui shrieked as he grew and swooped down from his perch, targeting the dark elf with a flame burst.

Kiera was knocked to the ground with a thud by Pryderi's body. And Shui's flames bounced off Donnagan's own shield.

"But dragon fire burns through everything," Cerys muttered in astonishment.

"So you brought friends. Not as foolish as I thought," Donnagan sneered readying another blast.

Sensing the building energy, and fearing for the lives of both her father and mate, Kiera transported herself into the line of fire. A white glow flecked with green shone all around her.

"You shall harm none," Kiera yelled as a purple bolt began to travel towards her.

Kiera's own white and green blast had been fired as she spoke, and it met the purple one. Her magick travelled along his energy path back to its owner, using his own flow to bypass the daoi-sith's defences. Donnagan was knocked off his feet, his body thumping against the ground.

"Now," Kiera shouted.

Frydah and Colle lit the area around the dark elf with intensely bright faery lights. Shui recouped his energy, and lit a ring of bright dragon fire around the dark elf's barrier. The daoi-sith's arm shot up to defend his eyes as he was blinded and weakened by the light.

Cerys and Chen intensified their shield around the area, blocking Donnagan's escape. Kiera, Threaris and Frydah issued the ear defender spell Kiera had benefited from at the ball, as Zondra sprang up, shrieking.

The noise was deafening, making Donnagan yelp in agony, unable to cover his eyes and ears at the same time. He was blind or deaf whatever he tried, and couldn't stop either assault very well. The combination of both was sapping his energy.

Donnagan couldn't concentrate. The pain piercing his eyes and ears was intense. He struggled to reach out to his magick.

'*Kiera's jewellery's glowing again,*' Frydah warned her friends telepathically.

Having seen his daughter's clever tactic, Threaris quickly zapped his blue magick to the purple one leaving Donnagan's hand.

The dark elf was trying to aim for Zondra to stop her racket. The sorcerer was the stronger of the two, and the blast sent the daoi-sith flying backwards, regrettably outside the ring of fire. He laughed maniacally as he found a possible route to freedom.

But Kiera zapped him too, knocking him into the cave's rocky entrance before he had the chance to transport himself. The force of the impact snapped his head back with a crack.

Seeing his mate in danger, Pryderi had launched himself at the dark elf with a howl.

"Pryderi, no," Kiera screamed, but too late, and her mate could not hear her.

Zondra was still screeching. Shui had lit another fire and the faeries had sent their lights nearer their foe. He was unable to fully maintain his defences and attack at the same time. He was vulnerable.

Dodging the dragon fire, Pryderi pounced on his prey. His jet amulet protected him from any residual defence the dark elf still had.

With a sickening crunch, Pryderi twisted Donnagan's head in his hands. His lifeless body slumped to the ground.

Chapter 29 – Cleansing

Everything fell silent. Everyone gazed at the corpse, not knowing what to do. It had all happened so suddenly. They had fulfilled their purpose, but felt nothing but sorrow. The daoi-sith was truly dead; Donnagan and his entire race.

The enormity of what they'd done hit them all. Never again would dark elves roam any realm.

Their quiet contemplation was interrupted by the beating of hooves.

"What have you done?" a shocked imperious voice broke the silence.

"What was needed and nothing more," Threaris stated simply, not looking up.

Queen Una flew down from her unicorn escort, and towards the lifeless body. In the human realm she appeared as small as any other faery.

"No!"

Frydah and Colle flew to their queen.

"He was given more than one chance. Even today, Kiera offered help, but he would not repent and showed no remorse," Frydah said softly.

"Look about you. Is any one of us rejoicing in this? Is there evil intent in any of us?" Kiera asked the queen.

"You don't understand. He held the darkness," she whimpered, looking all about her.

"Yes, all the darkness of his race. It was too much for one being to contain," Threaris stated.

"I was going to help him share his burden. I hoped a light elf may have bonded with him."

"He was incapable of feeling love, Queen Una. The light elf would have been tortured, and eventually would have died by his hand. It would never have been possible," Frydah explained.

"I could have tried," she cried, kneeling on the ground with the force of her despair.

"Oh goddess help us," Cerys muttered aside.

Threaris knelt beside the faery queen and placed a finger on her tiny arm.

"I did try. You know I did. You know the light elves failed in their efforts to bring him into the light. You know the evil atrocities which resulted from my failed attempt."

"But what will happen to all that dark energy now?"

More hoof beats thundered, signalling the approach of another.

"Cerys, why did you not call sooner?" a Welsh female voice questioned.

Everyone, even Shui and the unicorn, knelt and bent their heads to the goddess who had appeared amongst them.

"My apologies," Cerys offered awkwardly.

Rhiannon dismounted her trusty steed, and approached the sorry scene, her long green skirt and auburn hair fluttering in the wind.

"Ummm, Annie?" Kiera asked, her face scrunching up.

"I am sorry, dear child. Yes, you know me as Annie. The others here recognise me as the goddess Rhiannon."

"What? But what?" Kiered stammered.

"I didn't have chance to explain," Cerys apologised to them both.

"Time for that later. There is healing to be done here," Rhiannon stated.

The goddess looked towards the faery queen.

"Will you allow me?" she asked the tiny being.

The queen nodded sadly. Rhiannon touched a finger to Una's head and the faery began to grow.

"That's better. I can see you now."

Queen Una still had trails of tears running down her face, and her white hair clung to the moisture on her cheeks.

"These people speak true. There really was nothing else to do. Search your heart and you will see. Cleansing the energy will be done by me," the goddess told her.

Rhiannon turned to the gathered beings. "This energy is too dark, and must be cleansed. It does not belong here. I must make amends. The human realm has more than enough darkness without this to bear."

"Cerys, do you have black salt about your person?" the goddess asked.

"Of course," she said pulling a pouch out of her bag and offering it.

"Please scatter it in a circle around this unfortunate soul."

Cerys carried out her task with great solemnity, whilst Rhiannon comforted Una, bringing her to peace. Her birds flew down and offered their song to aid the process.

The team were jostled into a circle around the corpse, their heads bowed in respect to the passing of a life, no matter how evil it had been. The wind whipped up around them as Rhiannon began her ritual.

"Could I request your assistance, please?" she asked Shui.

The dragon breathed out his fire, starting a funeral pyre. Dark smoke curled and coiled up from the smouldering body. Rhiannon chanted, and the smoke turned dark grey, light grey then white. The wind carried the purified smoke upwards and away.

Each being wept. The couples held each other in comfort.

"Cerys, there are also herbs in your bag?" Rhiannon questioned.

"Always."

Herbs were handed around the circle to each mourner. Each person present scattered bay leaves, rosemary, sage and thyme onto the fire.

With the flames purifying the dark elf, Rhiannon recited, "As the energy has been cleansed so may the body and soul. May Donnagan find peace in the afterlife and be reborn anew. As above so below, as within so without. Blessed be."

They stood in respectful silence as the fire burned away all that once was Donnagan. Shui extinguished the flames when the funeral was complete.

There was a moment of awkward silence as the group debated internally as to what each should do next. Shock still hung around them like a cloak. Their fight was over.

Queen Una was the first to make her move, and quietly made her way home. She rarely left the fae realm and really shouldn't be away for long. Besides, there was nothing to do in this situation. She silently left with her unicorn, to make peace with what had transpired here.

Kiera was sobbing into Pryderi's shoulder. As reality sunk in, relief then guilt overcame her. She was relieved Donnagan was no longer a threat, but felt guilty that meant his life had been forfeit. No matter how much she told herself it was the only solution, remorse still twisted her gut.

Death was so final. And now a whole race had been eradicated. She felt responsible. OK, the race was an evil one who only brought chaos and devastation. But by killing Donnagan was she now no better than the daoi-sith?

"Pardon my intrusion. Your thoughts were loud, dear one. But this was not of your doing, you know. And the fact you are even asking yourself these questions shows how good you truly are. Do you think any daoi-sith ever considered their victims?" Rhiannon soothed.

"Perhaps not," Kiera replied, wiping her eyes, and looking up at the goddess.

"When the dark energy was expelled from the fae realm it was sent via those elves. A team had been tasked with the mission of taking it to other realms to cleanse and disperse it. Any energy which could not be cleansed was to be given unto the care of those who could deal with it properly."

"So they were light elves once too?"

"No. They were always dark. That is why it was thought they would be able to handle it. They had a sort of immunity to the darkness. But sadly it ensnared them, its power lulling them into its bidding. They used it, magnified it, and unleashed fury unto the human realm. Humans are still suffering now from the aftermath. But there are lightworkers restoring the balance. It is a long, slow process."

"Well that explains a lot."

Rhiannon merely smiled kindly as Kiera thought about the people humans grown up with; the volatile race she'd known. Pryderi's hand was rubbing Kiera's back, and his loving lips brushed the top of her head.

"This was always going to happen, wasn't it?" Kiera asked Rhiannon, her dewy eyes looking up at the goddess.

"From the moment the daoi-sith made their terrible choice."

"Thank you. I think that makes me feel a little better."

"I am glad of it," Rhiannon said with a smile and a dip of her head.

Taking hold of Pryderi's hand, Kiera suddenly exclaimed, "With no dark elf in our way nothing can stop us now."

"Kiera, no. Wait," Threaris shouted too late.

Kiera and Pryderi had disappeared.

Chapter 30 – Declaration

Kiera's friends all reacted immediately, following her in a heartbeat. The goddess was warmed by the love that she felt in the group. They were all loyal to one another. The kind of loyalty which was hard won in the face of adversity.

She however, had to be more subtle, not willing to announce her presence to a whole clan of elinefae.

Kiera appeared with Pryderi in the clan's large meeting space. The alarm went up immediately, and Rhion stormed in, followed by a large crowd of curious clan members.

"*I told you to stay away,*" he roared in Eline, "*You have disobeyed a direct order.*"

Kiera was aghast. Frydah was hovering at her side, throwing out as many protection spells as she could muster.

"Kiera, this is not a human faery tale. The elf's magick does not die with him," she managed to explain.

"What? But...?"

Pryderi was holding Kiera's hand tightly.

Turning to her he asked, "Is this what you thought?"

"Yes," Kiera admitted, staring at the ground, blushing.

Threaris was holding the angry Leader back with a spell of his own, which was making him angrier, but away from the treacherous pair.

Pryderi faced Rhion on bended knee.

"Sir, there is clearly a grave misunderstanding here."

"There certainly is. I have been weak allowing you both to live."

Threaris raised his hand to halt the Leader before he could make his declaration. Most of Kiera's friends all stiffened behind her, preparing to fight. Shui let out a warning growl.

"This is my clan. I will not be dictated to," Rhion bellowed.

"No, but you will listen before making a decision," Threaris told him firmly.

Cerys came rushing along, having made a quick stop at her den. In her hands was a crystal singing bowl with flecks of silver running through it.

"Please, let me make communication easier," she asked Rhion, not really caring for his response.

"Fine," he assented with a curl of his lip.

Cerys started running a wand around the bowl, making it sing. Everyone in the room was silenced as the deep sound built to Cerys' touch. She held the vibrating handle to Kiera's third eye, her heart, then her throat chakras, whilst murmuring a chant under her breath.

"Speak in your own tongue into the bowl," she demanded of Pryderi.

He said a few words in Eline as directed. Cerys held the bowl back to Kiera's throat until the vibrations and sound died away.

Kiera blinked before asking, "*What just happened?*"

Frydah was giggling into her hands. "You spoke Eline."

"*Yes, she's a genius. Can we please proceed?*" Rhion hissed.

Most of the clan were now gathered. Rumour had spread quickly of Kiera's presence, and of an ensuing fight. Amongst the chaos, Pryderi gave a quick bow to his Leader, and placed his fist on his heart.

"*Sir, we have overcome the threat of the daoi-sith. Thanks to Kiera we were able to capture him and subsequently end his life.*"

"*All I hear is you went outside clan without my permission,*" Rhion admonished.

"*But you were concerned with the threat. Surely you can see she was instrumental in helping?*" Pryderi replied, his mouth falling open.

"*No!*" The shout from the crowd made everyone freeze.

Arwyn marched forwards and up to the arguing males.

"*I will stand by and watch this no longer. I have seen my brother suffer more pain at your hands than any of our enemies ever inflicted,*" he growled at Rhion.

"*How dare you speak to me thus?*"

"*How dare I?*" he asked, glaring Rhion in the eyes, his face uncomfortably close, "*How dare you? You are our Leader and should be showing us the way. You declare Kiera would bring great danger to our clan, but I only see that she has saved us and other clans from our foes.*"

Rhion squared his shoulders and snarled, "*You would challenge me?*"

"*I never thought to say it, but yes. I am pledged to clan. My clan is made weaker of late by your actions. Yes, I challenge you.*"

Teeth were bared, the fight escalating more rapidly than anyone thought possible. A leadership challenge was being laid down. This had not happened in recent elinefae history. Even Dougal had stepped down gracefully as Leader of the Scottish clan, once he'd realised how he'd been led by a dark influence.

"*Enough,*" Kiera announced as she parted the pair, with both her magick and her physical presence, "*I will not be the cause of any dispute within any clan.*"

Before she could say anything further, a little lark who had been watching from the beams flew down, and hopped at Kiera's feet, chirruping. It flew up to her hip pouch and pecked at it until Kiera reached her hand down.

The lark landed back at her feet and watched intently, as Kiera delved into the bag, surprised at the bird's actions. She had learned it was better to go with the flow when strange things happened. This curious creature was obviously trying to tell her something, so she did her best to listen.

Her fingers touched the forgotten glass vial in her bag. She still wasn't entirely sure what it was, but the light elves had told her it would help against the daoi-sith. Biting her lip, she pulled the vial from her bag, hoping it would help this situation, and that she wasn't about to unleash something awful at the Leader.

"Oh yes, pull the stopper out and hold onto the bottle tightly," Frydah said excitedly at her side.

With a squeaky pop, the lid came off as Kiera tugged it. You could've heard a mouse fart as everyone watched on, afraid yet intrigued. They were watching a sorceress after all. One their Leader had been completely against.

Her father was standing to one side, a curious smirk playing across his lips, and a glint in his eyes. Zondra was next to him, also looking oddly amused.

The bottle was shaking in Kiera's hand and the clear fluid began to bubble. She firmed her grip, ensuring the vial didn't drop from her hands.

Small fingers of black mist started to creep out of the top of Rhion's head. They floated towards the vial in Kiera's grasp. It spiralled down into the opening and hit the liquid with a fizz.

More and more darkness travelled along the route set by the initial drawn energy. Kiera didn't know how it would all fit in, but it unfeasibly did. It looked like black oil was sitting on top of water inside the vial. At last, the thick dense dark tendrils became finer again and trailed into nothingness.

"Quick, put the top back on," Frydah instructed.

Kiera obeyed, squeezing the stopper back into place.

"Now shake it," Frydah said, grinning.

As Kiera shook the vial, the darkness mixed with the fluid. At first everything inside turned black before bubbling into dark blue, then grey. Eventually the liquid returned to its transparent state.

'Kiera, a word of warning. Donnagan used Rhion's existing prejudice. Your path is not yet as clear as that liquid,' her father warned her telepathically.

Rhion stood looking dazed and confused; his eyes wide, and was swaying on his feet. One of the Watchers placed a stool behind him, gently touching his shoulder, encouraging him to sink down onto the seat.

"*Your Leader has been under the influence of the daoi-sith which we have now vanquished*," Threaris announced to the clan, stepping forwards, "*I would ask that you do not judge him harshly for this. Even the best of us were susceptible to his cunning.*"

Kiera knelt in front of Rhion, and softly asked, "*Do you remember all that has been said here today?*"

"*Yes,*" he said, his eyes flickering.

"*Would you like some time to consider?*" she asked.

The Leader rose on shaky legs, and announced, "*I will indeed take time to reflect upon all this.*"

"*Please may we stay whilst you do?*"

He narrowed his eyes at her, but nodded with a huffed breath as he made his way to his private chamber. Cerys discreetly following behind.

In a moment of clarity, Kiera lifted her hands to cover her mouth. "Frydah, was I not supposed to use that on Donnagan? What if I could have helped him and spared his life?"

Her father had approached and replied instead of the faery, "It would have done no good. You may have been able to draw enough energy from him to weaken him so you could do the deed. The immense amount of darkness which was contained within him would not have fitted inside that vial. Please do not trouble yourself."

He gave her a quick reassuring hug, but retreated as braver members of the clan approached Kiera.

"*May I pet your dragon?*" one of the younglings asked her.

"*He is not mine. He is Chen's familiar.*"

The now dog-sized dragon padded up of his own accord, and offered his head forwards to the inquisitive child. She tentatively reached out her hand and stroked his nose.

Others soon joined, and there was a petting session until Shui off to hide behind Chen. The witch chuckled at his 'brave' friend.

Adults were quizzing Kiera, asking her who she was, and where she came from. Pryderi was proudly at her side, silently offering his support.

One youngling waggled a finger at Kiera, beckoning her down to her level. Kiera crouched down as instructed. The young girl looked at Kiera carefully.

"*I think you're elinefae,*" she declared after much deliberation and a big breath in.

"*Thank you. That's because I am,*" she replied with a small giggle.

"*You are clan,*" the child clarified.

"*Thank you. We shall see when your Leader returns,*" Kiera said around a lump in her throat.

The girl's mother had called her unruly child back to her side.

"Pardon my daughter. She is impulsive," the mother apologised.

"There is nothing to forgive," Kiera replied.

Kiera felt Pryderi's hand around her waist and his lips on her cheek as a couple approached them.

'My parents,' he told her inwardly.

Kiera was glad he'd told her. They didn't look much older than Pryderi himself.

"Hello. My name is Owen. I am Pryderi's father. It is nice to meet you at last," the kind-looking man said, leaning in, rubbing cheek to cheek.

Kiera sensed his signature; the scent of sandalwood filled her nose as she envisioned a black panther similar to Pryderi's. She distinctly saw the likeness between the two males.

She soon found herself wrapped in Pryderi's mother's arms and receiving another cheek rub.

"I am Eirlys," she greeted.

This female's signature scent echoed her name. Kiera sensed snowdrops from her, along with an image of a white tiger.

"Hello," Kiera smiled nervously with a curtsey to the pair.

She was slightly taken aback by their warm reception, having expected them to be cold and distant, under the command of their Leader still.

As if reading her mind, Eirlys softly told her, "*I do hope Rhion returns soon with a pleasing decision. It is wrong for you to be parted. Just one look tells of your status as a soul matched mated pair.*"

"*Thank you. I hope for good news too,*" Kiera replied, biting her lip and fidgeting.

"*You should never have been parted,*" the lovely lady told her, clasping Kiera's hands in her own.

***

Cerys was busy in the small room with Rhion, who was sitting down. She smudged his aura and spoke to him.

"*The law was put in place to protect from disease though. This was from the human DNA which had mixed in. Kiera is not human. Her sorceress blood should only strengthen your clan,*" she explained again, trying to be patient.

"*If I bend the rules for her what next?*"

"*You have a queue of clan members with mates from other races, do you?*"

"*No, but...*"

"But nothing. Kiera is a particular case. A one off. I don't think sorcerers make a habit of mating with elinefae, do you?" she asked, her arms crossed over her chest.

"Maybe not, but..."

"There's that word again. There is no but. You know the right of this, Rhion. Look at them. Just look. They are a soul matched mated pair. Would the goddess allow this if it was harmful?" Her arms unfolded, and her hands swept out, showing her palms.

"Well no, she would not."

"There we are then. Stop being twp and give your blessing. She will be an asset to your clan and bring you all honour."

"Will I not appear weak if I go back on my order?"

"You were under Donnagan's spell."

"Not entirely," he told her, looking up sideways.

"Oh, they don't need to know that. Yes, he used your own stubborn foolish notions against you. If you had met her without his interference I have every faith you would have acted differently."

The Leader smiled at his witch as he asked, *"You have faith in me?"*

"Do you have reason I should not?"

"I have acted dishonourably. I have been foolish."

"We can't hold stupidity against our friends now, can we? Otherwise we would have no friends left," she replied with a wink.

"Friends. You still call me this?"

Cerys ruffled the Leader's hair as she confirmed, *"Of course, you fool male. I'm just glad you are you again."*

"Me too. Many thanks for your assistance, as always, Cerys."

"You are more than welcome. Come, are you ready?"

Nodding, he rose to his feet. Cerys planted a kiss on his cheek, making him smile down at her.

***

A loud scuffling sounded as the clan shuffled backwards when two Watchers appeared, preparing for Rhion's re-entrance. Silence fell all around.

Kiera felt like she may wet herself. She was unaware of what had just transpired. Pryderi's arm was thankfully still around her waist, helping her to remain standing on her wobbly legs.

Her mate kissed the top of her head, holding her close, no doubt feeling just as nervous as her. If his Leader still denied their coupling he may well pronounce their death warrant this time.

Their friends rallied around behind them, readying themselves for the worst, but hoping for the best. Kiera and Pryderi knew they would be protected whatever the decision, but feared a fight would ensue. They didn't want to be the cause of any more animosity.

The whole audience held their silence as the Leader entered the meeting space, tall and proud. Taking large confident strides, he approached the petrified pair. Threaris shifted his position, his fingers drumming the air by his side, his eyes locked onto his target.

Yellow beady eyes stared down at Kiera and Pryderi, as if the Leader was looking at them together for the first time.

"*It seems I have been influenced by dark forces,*" Rhion mumbled through his red bushy beard, before clearing his throat.

"*I have not acted as I should. For this I apologise,*" he announced more clearly.

The couple stood motionless, holding their breath in anticipation. It was still unclear to them which way this decision would go.

"*Yet Kiera remains a halfling.*"

Zondra held Threaris back as his arm began to rise.

There was a stirring behind the pair too, as their friends readied for an attack. And there were groans and murmurings of dissent from the gathering of elinefae.

Rhion held his hand up to silence them all.

"It remains a fact. And one which until now would have led to her execution."

Growls and hisses echoed around, and the room seemed to grow smaller as everyone surged forwards. Kiera buried her head in Pryderi's chest as he held her close, glaring over her head in defiance at his Leader.

Rhion raised his voice above the din, and quickly continued, *"However, being half sorceress and not human changes things. This has never been seen before. Kiera has shown this blending has strengthened her, and she has indeed helped broker peace between two warring clans."*

Silence filled the space as the clan collectively held their breath.

"She has proven herself honest, true and brave. She has assisted in the eradication of the dark elf who not only plagued me, but also her own father. I am sure she will be an asset to our clan."

Cheers erupted in the room and feet thumped the ground as people jumped for joy.

"Kiera, Kiera," they chanted clamorously.

Rhion stepped forwards to shake Kiera's hand. Bowing her head, she received his cheek rub.

"*Welcome to our clan,*" he announced loudly as he gripped her upper arm.

She winced slightly as a stinging sensation pricked under his touch. Her lip curled as she tried to decide what he was doing.

As he took his hand away she noticed a mark on her skin. A Trinity Knot with dragon heads and green highlights had appeared on her arm, just like Pryderi's.

"Look, I'm like you," she exclaimed to Pryderi.

His fingers were hiding his smile and he subtly nodded at his mate.

"*Of course. You are clan. My mate. Family,*" he purred.

Chapter 31 – Lust for Life

Pryderi and Kiera were provided with a den in the couples section of the clan. Cerys and Frydah helped to decorate so it was more homely for Kiera. Elinefae life was a lot more basic than the one she was used to.

There was a large wooden four poster bed, with intricate carvings, and a big comfy mattress on top. Bouncing as she sat, Kiera gave it a quick test, thrilled with her luxurious gift.

There was also a large wardrobe. Peering inside, Kiera found replicas of her elinefae styled outfit, as well as some more casual elinefae garments. Pryderi's clothes were next to hers. She grinned from ear to ear.

Cerys pointed upwards. Kiera didn't think she could smile any more, but somehow her mouth broadened as she saw the skylight Cerys had installed. There was a shaft of light coming into the room.

Most dens were enclosed, which Kiera would have felt claustrophobic in. Kiera would be able to see the sun or the stars through the skylight, making the room feel less cave like.

"*It's concealed, you can't see it from the outside,*" Cerys reassured Pryderi, who also thanked her.

Under the beam of light was a small stand. Kiera saw her beloved iPod sitting on top.

"But how will I recharge it?" she asked.

"Look again," Cerys told her.

The witch had created a solar powered charger, which was sitting in the light.

Kiera grabbed the witch in a bear hug.

"Thank you so much," she cried, her tears of joy flowing unchecked.

"I helped too," Frydah said, clapping her hands.

Faery lights lit up around the bed at the sound of her claps.

"Oh, they're beautiful. Thank you," Kiera sobbed, holding her cheek out to her faery friend to cling to.

"*It's perfect. Thank you all so much,*" she blubbed.

"*Anything to make you happy,*" Pryderi whispered as he wrapped his arms around her.

She clung onto him tightly, using him as an anchor to her safety and happiness.

"*I really am home, aren't I?*" she said through her tears.

"*You were from the first moment I kissed you,*" he told her, his voice gravelled.

The pair were left alone so they could mark their room as their own. As they made love their scent strengthened and permeated the den.

***

Over time, Kiera began to settle into her new surroundings. She joined Pryderi on his Watcher patrols, only partially due to being unable to bear parting from him.

She had seen the area where they grew vegetables, and learned of their irrigation system. Water poured out of a small tunnel which led down from the latrines. Rain water was collected and mixed with the sewage, which then fertilised their own crops. This was well out of eyesight from any strangers, who would not be able to cross their barrier.

Kiera learned that people would unwittingly avoid the area around the barrier, not even aware of why. The magick truly protected her new home. She was safe.

Pride swelled in her bosom as she learned how ecological her family were. They wouldn't even think to give their lifestyle a name. It was just life to them. For a moment, she wished humans could see them, just so they could learn how to honour their planet.

The sun was shining through the clouds, making her smile. She was starting to appreciate this place, and was beginning to believe things would be alright after all.

Near the end of one of their patrols, Kiera breathed in the smells of the forest, and felt her tensions ease. It was as if a weight had been lifted. She remained silent for a long time, her mind trying to process all that had happened.

Her life had been turned upside down, and she'd been left feeling dizzy and confused at first. She bit her lip as she realised how much she'd faced and overcome. Her mate licked her lips, bringing her out of her reverie.

"Sorry, I was doing it again wasn't I?" she asked, realising her lip biting had become a habit.

"It tastes good though."

"What does?"

"Sometimes your fangs dig in. A small spot of blood is left before you heal."

"Ah, that's why you keep stopping me with your tongue?"

He nodded, smiling bashfully.

"I still can't believe I'm here."

"It is where you belong," he whispered, taking her face in his hand.

"But it wasn't. I was brought up amongst humans. I never knew this world existed. And then there was my kidnapping, and my father, and the clan battle, and Donnagan, and Rhion," she listed with tears threatening.

"Shh, all that is in the past. You are here now," he told her, moving in for a kiss.

"I'm different still though."

"Better."

"You don't really believe that?"

"Don't I, Kiera?" he smiled releasing a sexy heavy breath, looking into her glistening green eyes.

She shook her head, butterflies fluttering in her tummy. He looked and sounded so hot like that. Biting her lip, she tried to concentrate on calming her rising libido.

"You really must stop this, or I will pounce here and now," he warned, lapping her mouth.

Her answering giggle was cut off as his mouth descended over hers. Heat swelled her nub, shooting fire up her core.

He let her feel the full force of his lust as their kiss deepened. He ground his hips against her body. In answer, her leg lifted against his, trying to get more purchase. Her hands were exploring his back, drawing him in.

Smelling her arousal, and feeling she was ready, he moved away abruptly, making her grunt in frustration.

"Come, I wish to show you something," he whispered seductively.

"Can't you show me here?" she whined.

"You'll like it."

"But we have patrol."

"It is safe. Come on," he said, pulling her in the direction he wanted them to go in.

Resigning herself to his whim, she followed Pryderi back through the quiet camp, and along the maze of dimly lit tunnels. He stopped outside a door she was unfamiliar with.

"Before we go in, I need you to know nobody else will touch you," he assured her.

"What? Pryderi, what are we doing?"

"Other couples can mingle, and singles meet others to satisfy their needs. But you and I are bound to each other. We are meant only for each other."

"Pryderi, you're worrying me," she warned, a frown creasing her forehead.

"We can hear others. But we also feel their emotions too. You have felt this already."

"Yes," she said, drawing out the word.

"Please, let me share this with you."

She was biting her lip again. Pryderi dipped his head down to suck that lip free. His tongue licked the edge of her gum line.

He moved his mouth to her ear, where he licked its outer edges before blowing softly. The ensuing tingles shot through Kiera's entire body, straight to her groin.

As he continued to nip and blow, the warmth spread, and the moistness grew between her legs.

He opened the door.

'*Welcome to the den of sin,*' he told her mind-to-mind.

Kiera gasped as she noticed naked bodies writhing in the red glow of the room.

'Pryderi, what are you doing? I can't see,' she complained nervously, squinting.

'The light in here gives privacy,' he informed her, *'Open your feelings out. Can you feel them?'*

Taking a deep breath in, she felt the lust wash over her. It was mingled with her own, and threatened to engulf her. The desire which had been building, was now a deep seated need.

Pryderi led his mate to an empty bench in the corner. He slowly undressed her, tantalisingly slowly. Her breath hitched with every move he made.

Guiding her feet up onto the bench, so she was standing taller than him, he put one of her hands on a bar above her head on the wall. She instinctively held on with her other hand too, putting all her faith in him.

His mouth suckled on one of her nipples, drawing out a groan of pleasure from her. His own eyes glowed brightly in the dim red light. He nipped and licked his way down her torso, sending shivers up her spine.

Someone else in the room reached their climax, sending waves of lust through Kiera and Pryderi. It drove her wild, and she grabbed Pryderi's head to where she needed him to be.

Obeying her directions, Pryderi licked along the edges of her folds. Kiera wriggled.

'Please,' she urged him.

He brought one of her feet over his shoulder, the other dutifully following. With her legs spread around his neck he licked along the full length of her slit, pausing at her nub to suck hard.

Kiera was sent reeling into her orgasm, her hips bucking to meet his mouth. She was hanging off the bar above her, Pryderi holding her buttocks in support.

Groans echoed around the room as others felt the passion saturate them.

"I need to feel you," she groaned out loud.

Helping her put her feet back on the bench, he lowered her onto the little step in front of it.

Kiera was now facing the wall, and Pryderi nudged her feet with his to widen her stance.

His erection was at her rear as he stepped in closely. She wriggled her bum, trying to entice him in, needing inside her.

Instead, he reached a hand around her hips and rubbed where he'd been licking.

"Fuck me," she spat through gritted teeth, unable to bear any further torment.

Sighing ecstasy, she felt his hard cock slide inside her, long and slow. He filled her. But still she needed more.

Swaying her hips back and forth, he could deny her no longer. He thrust in and out of her warm wetness.

Another couple screamed out their orgasm, bringing Kiera closer to another release.

Pryderi reached up and around to massage her breasts, making her moan. As he tugged her nipple she came apart around him.

Her muscles clenched tightly around his cock as she thrust her hips back and forth, milking him with all her might. She screamed her delight through the darkness, taking Pryderi through to his own release.

He thrust harder and faster, pounding into her, roaring his pleasure as he filled her with pleasure.

Similar roars shot out around them in the dark red glow.

They stood still a moment to catch their breath before uncoupling and collapsing onto the bench.

Pryderi sat with his back against the wall, whilst Kiera sat astride his lap to kiss him deeply, her hands roughly combing through his shaggy hair.

'Steady tiger,' he silently warned her.

But she couldn't heed his warning. Still needing him, she was overcome with the desire chasing around the room.

The scent of their arousal mingled with the electricity she felt tingling across her skin. Her magickal bouquet and his spicy forest scents intensified as they intertwined with a salty tang. Their aroma was so strong she could taste it. All her senses were bombarded with pure desire.

She grabbed hold of his cock, stroking its slippery length back to attention. Mounting him in one swift move, she started pumping up and down, gripping onto his hair at the back of his head.

He was breathless with desire, only able to gulp short bursts of air as his mate rode him into oblivion.

Their bodies were glistening with sweat as she continued her onslaught.

He gripped her buttocks to assist her up and down movements.

She threw her head back as another orgasm ripped through her, shooting stars into the darkness of her mind.

With a few more thrusts, Pryderi was completely undone, and found home in her depths. He bit into her shoulder as he came hard inside her. Her blood trickling down his throat.

She screamed with him as they rode the final wave together.

He lapped at the love bite he'd given her, healing it instantly.

Kiera wrapped her arms around her lover's neck as she trailed kisses along his cheeks, and nestled into his neck, mewling her satisfaction against his skin.

Their breathing slowed as they surfaced for air.

'I think we need to get out of here,' he told her quietly.

"Uh uh," she groaned before zapping them to their den, not forgetting to include their clothing.

Pryderi looked down into his mate's eyes, and saw them trying to close.

"Tired now?" he smiled at her lazily.

"Uh huh," she moaned.

He laid her down on their bed and spooned against her, thanking the goddess for blessing him with such a magnificent mate.

Chapter 32 – Meetings

When Kiera finally woke up she still felt groggy, but found her mate nuzzling her neck.

"Morning, sleepy head," he smiled, nudging her with his nose.

"Morning."

"Happy?" he asked.

"Mmm," she moaned with pleasure as she stretched, "Blissfully."

"Good," he said, twisting her round so they could rub noses.

"So what do we do now?" she asked dreamily.

"What would you like to do?"

She wiggled her eyebrows at him suggestively.

"Really?"

She laughed. "No. I don't have the energy after my stint with sin. Why is it called the den of sin anyway? It felt heavenly to me."

He rubbed noses again as he told her, "I'm glad you enjoyed it. I know you were brought up in a different world. It is so named because Cerys saw it one day. She hurried past shaking her head, muttering it was a den of sin. The name stuck. Someone asked her what sin was. We laughed so hard we cried when we discovered its meaning."

Kiera laughed. "You didn't know what sin was?"

He shook his head.

"Hmm, I suppose you wouldn't. You're not religious in that way, are you?"

"Not like humans, no. The Earth is our Mother. We have right from wrong. But sin is an odd thing. Especially about sex. How can an act of love be wrong?"

"I couldn't agree more," she said, stretching again.

"Of course, it is not just love expressed there."

"It felt that way to me."

He playfully poked her nose as he told her, "It would, my mate. But all elinefae feel deep desires. Our blood runs high. Sometimes it is pure lust. Single elinefae have a place to release that."

"No strings attached?"

"No, it is just sex for them," he told her with a shrug.

"But not for you?"

"Not for us," he corrected.

A deep rumble echoed around their den.

"Was that you?" he asked, grinning, staring at her stomach.

She nodded bashfully.

"Let us see what food there is then."

She marvelled at the simplicity here. You're hungry, you find food. You lust, you have sex. There was nothing complicated.

They wandered happily together to the eating area.

"Ah, there they are," Arwyn cheered.

"We were missed?" Pryderi asked.

"You were not seen at the meal after patrol."

"Oh, we...err..." Kiera flustered.

"Relax, sister. I am teasing. We know why. But Rhion was looking for you."

"He was?" Pryderi asked, frowning.

"You should seek him out after patrol today. He is probably seeking his own bed now."

Pryderi nodded as he loaded his plate with bread for both himself and his mate.

"Do you want eggs today, princess?" he asked Kiera, ducking down at the fireside.

His nickname for her had begun on their first day together in the clan. She'd been like a fish out of water. There wasn't as much as a toaster, and she'd been shocked at the lack of appliances. When she explained her ways of making breakfast, he had told her she was like a princess living in luxury, like the fairytales he had heard as a youngling.

Receiving her smile and nod, he cracked their eggs into a pan, and set it on a stand over the fire as he toasted the bread on a fork held to the flames.

Kiera poured their coffee into cups and took them to the bench. She sat opposite Arwyn and Elan. This had already become their morning routine. She smiled at the familiarity of it.

Pryderi brought their food over and kissed his mate's cheek as he took his place at her side.

To their surprise, Rhion walked in.

"*Ah, there you are,*" he said as he approached them.

"*My apologies. I have only just been alerted you were looking for us, sir,*" Pryderi said, lowering his head.

Their relationship was still strained as they sought to repair the damage done by the daoi-sith.

One of the other Watchers passed a cup of coffee to the Leader. He paused to take a sip.

"*You have been summoned to coven, Kiera,*" Rhion told her, still pronouncing her name Hera with a throaty hiss.

"*Oh, but I am not a witch,*" she mumbled in response.

"*Nonetheless, the witches have requested your presence.*"

"*Of course, I shall be there,*" she accepted with a nod of her head.

Having delivered his message, the Leader stalked off.

Kiera had already visited her family clans in Ireland and Scotland in her short time here. She was unsure whether Rhion resented her time away from his clan, or whether he thought her unworthy of the attention. Either way, he was never impressed with her departure.

She briefly wondered why Cerys had not informed her of this particular visit, but then shrugged it off; the witch was going through the proper channels. Whether she got on with him or not, Rhion was now her Leader.

To be honest, Kiera was still uncomfortable being treated like some sort of celebrity, being paraded around. It was even worse now there was a starker contrast with the simplicity of her new life.

She was also a little homesick. She'd not been back to see her adoptive parents, and hoped to be able to see them soon. Of course, she'd have to use a glamour, but wanted their familiar hugs; something stable in amongst all this change.

When it was time for her to go to the coven, Kiera dressed in her long green cloak and placed her circlet on her cushion of hair. She begrudgingly kissed Pryderi goodbye. He had accompanied her on the other trips, but this was a sacred one, and he was not able to accompany her.

Transporting herself at the allotted time to the location she'd been given, she arrived to a crowd. All the witches had already convened, and the circle had been opened. Kiera could feel the buzz of their magick in the air, and felt its comfort wash through her. This place felt tranquil despite the murmurs coming from those present.

Cerys was leading this meeting, and beckoned Kiera over to stand with her.

"This is Kiera, who you've all heard so much about. I'm sure you all know she's now residing in Rhion's clan. She's even met a couple of you already," Cerys announced, looking pointedly at the witches from Kiera's family clans.

"Merry meet," echoed around the circle.

"Merry meet," Kiera replied, waving awkwardly.

Reaching out to shake the first hand offered to her, she found herself being drawn around the circle to shake hands with every witch there. Many of them peered from under their cloak hoods at her.

"You seem very young," one witch declared as Kiera reached her starting position.

"That is because I am. Is that a problem?" she challenged.

"I am merely uncertain on your experience and knowledge of our ways."

"Just because something has always been done a certain way does not mean it is right."

"So you're here to change things?"

"No. I merely wish to live my life with my clan."

"That seems like a waste of power," another witch grumbled.

"Yes, she has great power, and has shown she can use it wisely," the witch from Kiera's Irish clan spoke up for her.

"I have heard of your battle. My thanks go to this girl for her intervention. I am hopeful she may use her powers to assist us more."

"Can I not just live my life in peace?" Kiera asked.

"Peace should be available to all," another added, his hood nodding up and down.

"I thought the elinefae were at peace?" Kiera asked, her eyebrows crinkling.

"There are varying levels of peace, my dear," Cerys pointed out, standing at her side.

"Oh, well, of course I will do what I can to help."

"Then it is settled. I move to assign Kiera as elinefae Peacekeeper."

"I support that motion," another seconded.

"Then I suggest we vote on it. All those in favour of Kiera being appointed Peacekeeper light your candle now," Cerys declared.

With that many candles were lit in the centre of the circle. Only five remained unlit.

"Motion carried. Kiera, I officially bestow upon you title of Peacekeeper to the clans," Cerys announced as she placed a silver brooch, shaped like a dove, onto her cloak.

Kiera curtseyed and gave her thanks, but inside her thoughts were whirling. What had she just agreed to? What was expected of her now? She glowered at Cerys as she prepared to make her exit. Her friend made her promise to a conference with her at the earliest opportunity.

True to her word, Kiera hadn't transported herself home, but went straight to Cerys' cottage to await her so-called friend. The pair had serious words when Cerys and Chen returned. Kiera was very unhappy that she'd been railroaded into this new role.

But once Cerys explained the role, Kiera began to calm down. At the end of the day, she wanted her species to be happy. And if she could help she would. She still didn't appreciate the sneaky way Cerys had gone about it, but accepted her duties.

Over the next few months, Kiera's services were called on several times by other clans. She settled disputes which threatened to overspill to interclan brawls, and became respected amongst the elinefae and witches. She was always firm yet fair. Her outsider views often helped shed new light on situations, providing new solutions to old problems.

As her own reputation was elevated, so was her clan's by extension. Rhion was slowly beginning to see Kiera's true value.

Summer ended, and Samhain approached as the leaves turned orange, gold and brown. The celebration was very different from the one humans call Halloween. The clans were busy making preparations for the moment when all clans converged to celebrate together.

Pryderi had explained that the magick of the sabbat would summon the clans to another realm. This one didn't hold as much magick as the fae one, but more than the human world. It held the elinefae in safety as they were brought together in celebration of the harvest. Plus, it had the added benefit of guaranteeing them dry weather.

Witches and elinefae from all over the northern hemisphere gathered. The southern clans celebrated their Beltane weddings privately at this time.

The witching hour approached, and Kiera felt a buzz rush through her clan. It was like the electricity before a thunderstorm, but smelled like musty leaves and apples.

Carts had been loaded up with offerings and supplies. Kiera had been part of the massive hunt to capture as many deer as possible. Some were magickally stored for winter, and some were now loaded on one of the carts, along with apples, nuts, barrels of cider and the last of the fruits and berries.

A horn sounded, and the clan members stiffened slightly as they found themselves taken across to the other realm. Kiera held Pryderi's hand tightly. This wasn't like her usual transportation. It was slower, and she saw blurred fuzzy images of her clan as they were taken across.

Kiera blinked a few times to clear her vision, but then relaxed as she saw everyone was safe. Each clan was gathered in their own designated area of the massive gathering place. In the centre was a large altar. The witch from each clan, dressed in their finest robes, approached the altar, holding a cup. Sprinkling cider on the ground, they chanted:

"Summer is gone, winter is approaching.

The light is dimming and darkness is encroaching.

Our harvests we have sown and reaped.

To the goddess we ask our stores to keep."

Each of the clan Leaders then filed up to the altar, and placed an item of food or drink on it. Once every clan had placed their offering they gathered around and placed their hand to their hearts as they invoked:

"To the ancestors of our past,

we offer thanks and peace which lasts.

From them we receive and to them we give,

together this feast we share in order to live."

The Second of each clan then formed a torch-lit procession to light the bonfires. It became a free-for all as clan members all thronged to throw herbs on the sacred pyres.

Then it was time to party. All the clans mingled, seeking old friends and relatives in particular. Kiera found herself being pulled in all directions as her new friends called to her. Pryderi stuck by her side, beaming with pride at her acceptance amongst so many.

Shui had joined the party too. As Chen and Cerys managed to find Kiera in the middle of the crowd, Shui took flight.

His shrieking roar pierced the night, and silenced the crowd. Most elinefae hadn't seen a dragon before, and even Kiera's clan was slightly unnerved by his cry. The clans fled away from the noise, and therefore also from Kiera who stood still.

With a massive downdraft, an enormous shadow descended over the assembled guests. A deep roar rumbled through every body as an exceedingly large red Welsh dragon landed in the space which had been cleared. Gasps could be heard, and a few screams, but none felt able to move away any further.

Chen's dragon flew towards Kiera and clutched her arm gently with a claw, and pulled her closer to the newcomer. She had no option but to go with him. Pryderi followed close behind.

'Bow,' she heard Chen inform her telepathically.

Kneeling down on one knee, she bowed her head towards the giant dragon, her arms stretched out from her sides. To her surprise the large dragon stretched out his front legs and inclined his head to her.

Putting his head in close to hers, he sniffed in big, hot, puffy breaths. Kiera thought she could detect a smile as the dragon seemed to nod to an unasked question.

Slowly, the Welsh dragon uncurled his long tail, being careful not to hit any bystanders. As he did so, Kiera saw the egg he'd been holding within his coils. He nudged it towards Kiera.

Her mouth dropped open as she gasped. "For me?"

The dragon slowly nodded, and blinked its enormous black eyes. There was a strange rumbling noise, almost like a purr. With a final bow of its thick neck and heavy head, the dragon flapped its wings.

The crowd fell to the ground as wind and dust swept across them when the dragon's wings beat faster, before it took off into the night sky. Kiera was first to get to her feet, and watched in awe as the silhouetted figure disappeared into the distance. The moonlight just caught the tip of his left wing.

She heard a chirrup as Chen's dragon hopped towards her feet, and nudged the egg. Bending, Kiera picked up the precious treasure.

"I did not know there were any dragons left in Wales," Chen admitted, his mouth gaping, "Let alone a dragon lord."

"It's news to me too, but that was definitely a Welsh dragon, make no mistake," Cerys burst in.

"Dragon lord? Aren't they the humans who tame dragons?" Kiera asked, thinking back to the films she'd seen.

"Do not even think that. No. We can be custodians of dragons, and help them. But we are never their trainer. They are here to teach us," Chen replied angrily.

"Sorry. Please tell me. I clearly don't know."

"The lord of dragons is a dragon. He is a guardian, like the elinefae Leaders. He protects the dragons in his area."

"Oh," Kiera said.

"You have been given a great honour. They must trust you implicitly."

"Like they trust you?"

"No. I rescued Shui during battle. His mother was killed by those who should have known better. You have been given this gift."

"But I'm not a dragon. How do I hatch this, let alone look after it?"

Shui was dipping his head left to right, looking very pleased with himself.

"I think you will have help," Chen told her, jabbing a thumb in Shui's direction.

Stepping up to Shui, who was cat sized at that moment, he picked him up by the scruff of his neck.

"I cannot believe you did not tell me," he reprimanded lightly as he dangled the dragon at eye level.

Shui stuck his nose up in the air and shook his head as he screeched out a giggle.

"Huh, wanted to keep the surprise, eh?" Chen laughed as he put the dragon back down.

Shui shook himself, and shrank down so he could fly up to Chen's shoulder. The dragon received a head scratch from his companion, who could not be angry at his familiar.

Kiera and Chen found somewhere safe for the egg by a fire. Shui kept guard as the clans continued their Samhain celebrations.

Chapter 33 – Union

Kiera had to fit babysitting in along with her other duties. For the next five weeks, Frydah and Shui helped Kiera incubate and care for the small purple egg. Kiera carried it in a sling packed with straw when she was out of the den.

Finally one day, whilst patrolling the forest, there was a cracking sound. Kiera peered down at her precious cargo. A tiny beak of a nose started to peek through a crack in the egg.

Kiera sat down in the forest, calling Pryderi, Frydah and Shui to her. They all looked on as the tiny green baby dragon emerged as a hatchling, making gurgling growling sounds.

Shui quickly found some worms to offer the baby, who gobbled up the offering with great enthusiasm. Kiera remarked how surprised she was at its colour.

"What, you expected it to be purple with pink polka dots?" Frydah scoffed.

"Well no. But I did sort of think a purple dragon may come from a purple egg."

"Still so very human," Frydah said disdainfully, shaking her head.

"It's not as if I've witnessed any dragon births," Kiera retorted.

The dragon cried out, distracting the pair from their banter.

"Shui, please can you find him some more worms?"

Shui shook his head from side to side.

"No you won't fetch food?" she asked, shocked at his sudden neglect.

Shui gave her a wry dragon look and tapped one of his hind feet, showing his impatience.

"I think it may be a girl," Frydah said watching the hatchling.

Shui nodded before disappearing for more supplies.

"How can you tell?"

Putting her hand to the side of her mouth, Frydah whispered aside, "I can't. I was just guessing from Shui's look."

"I suppose I was too distracted to listen to his message."

The girls giggled as they petted the baby dragon's head.

"Shh, more food is on its way," Kiera soothed.

The hatchling cooed at her.

"So, what are we going to call our dragon daughter?" Pryderi asked, joining in the petting.

"Terrah," Kiera quickly blurted out.

The dragon looked up with her big black eyes, blinked and burbled happily.

"I think that's agreed," Pryderi smiled.

***

Terrah grew rapidly, and Shui helped to teach the baby dragony ways. She was an enthusiastic, boisterous little thing. Apart from being green and not red, she was also a different shape from Shui. She was stouter, and her already large wings which extended out from her back. Her snout was stubby, especially in comparison to her friend's long thin one. Her element was earth and not water. But they both breathed fire.

There was only one permanent scorch mark on Kiera and Pryderi's bed post. Dragon fire is incredibly powerful. It can do great good, but a toddler can inflict great damage in a tantrum. Kiera was lucky it hadn't been worse. Even she couldn't erase the mark. But she didn't really want to. It was a reminder to always respect dragons.

***

Not long after, Rhion had sought out Kiera and Pryderi before they started their duty for the day. He stomped towards them with confident strides.

"*Kiera, Pryderi, it seems to me you two are slow in announcing your hand-fasting.*"

Kiera noted he no longer hissed her name, but pronounced the hard K.

"*Sir?*" Pryderi checked in disbelief.

"*You heard. Good watch,*" he said as he walked off.

The pair were gobsmacked, as were their friends who were enjoying breakfast with them.

"I don't understand. What was that all about?" Kiera asked, using English in her confusion.

"*Hand-fasting is like your wedding, but only for soul matched mates,*" Pryderi explained.

"*It is a great commitment, and I think our Leader has just given you his blessing,*" Elan added.

Brushing Kiera's cheek with his hand, Pryderi asked, "*Do you want to go and speak with Cerys?*"

Kiera had initially spent quite a lot of time with Cerys, receiving instruction on elinefae life, and what was expected of her. The witch was happy to be her confidant and guide.

It was also a good opportunity to speak to her human parents on the telephone. She'd not forgotten them. She had created a cover story of going off travelling, which excused her physical presence. And she phoned from Cerys' house, hiding the number, to check in at regular intervals.

Now Kiera was nodding at her mate, glad of the excuse to chat with her friend. She hoped to catch Cerys before she went to her shop. Chen was always good, and held the fort when needed, but she didn't like to abuse his friendship.

As soon as she'd finished eating, Kiera bid her friends farewell, and, giving Pryderi a kiss, she transported herself to Cerys' cottage.

Chen was humming in the kitchen, preparing breakfast, so Kiera walked in through the backdoor.

The witch looked up at the sound of the chimes as she entered, and gave their visitor a broad grin. "Good morning."

"Morning, Chen. Is Cerys up and about?"

"She is just getting ready. Is everything alright?"

"I'm fine. Rhion just told us we should have a hand-fasting, and Pryderi said maybe I should speak with Cerys about it."

"Ah, I see. Well, as soon as I have eaten I will leave you to it."

"I'm sorry. I seem to keep chasing you away."

"Not at all. We both like being in the quiet of the shop. It is my honour to be there."

Lowering his voice conspiratorially, he said behind his hand, "And it gives me a chance for true quiet."

As if proving his point, Cerys came into the kitchen.

Seeing Kiera there, she screeched, "Morning dear, what a pleasure to see you. Are you OK?"

Kiera found herself wrapped up in the witch's arms.

Releasing herself from the tight hug, Kiera explained her reason for being there.

"Would you like breakfast, Kiera?" Chen asked.

"Oh no thank you. I've just eaten."

"You are sure? I made jiānbǐng."

"Oh, go on then," she accepted with a smile, unable to resist his tasty pancakes.

He dished up for the ladies, and grabbed his own portion to go.

Kissing Cerys on his way out the door, he cheerily said goodbye. Cerys was dewy eyed when she looked back at Kiera, who was glad to see her friend so happy.

"You make such a lovely couple," she couldn't resist commenting.

"Oh, off with you," Cerys dismissed with a wave of her hand.

Walking them through to the lounge so they could sit comfortably, Cerys smiled at Kiera.

"So, you are to have a hand-fasting, eh?"

"Yes. Well, I think so. Pryderi said it's like a wedding."

"Oh, it is. But a lot more serious. Only soul matched mated couples can enact the ritual in elinefae society. They take it most seriously."

"Weddings are serious." Kiera defended the human culture she was brought up with.

"Yes, but the elinefae one can never be broken. You and Pryderi are soul matched. You know how painful it is when you are separated for too long. So the ceremony is confirmation of this, but you are pledging your souls to one another in the name of the goddess."

Cerys continued to explain the process and what would be expected of Kiera.

"Well, I had better go find Chen before he thinks I've abandoned him," Cerys said as she stood.

The ladies were outside, Cerys locking her door the old fashioned way. The scent of azaleas wafted along, making Kiera inhale deeply.

"Mmmm, that scent is so amazingly sweet."

"Hm hmm, you should like it given your own scent, and the assistance that flower gave you," Cerys chuckled.

"Yes, I suppose so. Bless Azalea."

Kiera paused as a thought occurred to her.

"Your name isn't really Cerys, is it?"

The witch bristled and bustled, before clearing her throat enough to declare, "It is the name I answer to."

"Don't be coy. All witches have flowery names. But not you. Why?"

"I thought we were talking about azaleas and handfasting?" she tried to deflect.

"Yes, but it's just hit me. So, what is your name?"

"It means love. It was given to me as an honorary title."

"Your real name, Cerys?"

"Argh, it's Bougainvillea. There, are you happy now?"

Kiera giggled. "The one Hawaiians call devil flower because of its spines?"

"Oh, you're not good at gardening, but this you know?"

"I read about it in a romance novel once, and was intrigued. It sounded like it smelled wonderful. I looked it up."

"It is a symbol of protection and passion, thank you very much."

"Sorry," Kiera apologised, trying to keep a straight face, "So why change it?"

"It's a bit of a mouthful, and shortening it to Boogie is crass. Humans would never accept me with such an outrageous name. It gets associated with oogie boogie, which they think of as sinister. Besides, I can't get the bloody things to grow," she added in a huff.

"All very good reasons. I'm sorry, Cerys. I was just curious."

"Curiosity killed the cat."

"Haha, I say the exact same thing. It doesn't go down too well around the clan though," she admitted, pulling a face.

They both fell into laughter.

"Is it the same for Chen?"

"Oh no. His name really is Chen. The flower names is a British thing. Americans use trees and Chinese use the zodiac. Ironically, Chen is associated with the dragon. The fates have humour. It means great or morning, but do try to forget that. He doesn't need his head to swell any more."

The girls giggled as they parted ways.

***

The first of May arrived, bringing Beltane along with it; the time reserved for handfastings.

Frydah and Colle had helped make Kiera the most beautiful gown ever seen by elinefae kind.

The bodice was made of soft green moss, decorated with dew drops sparkling like diamonds. The attached full skirt was made of brown silk-like material, which apparently the spiders had spun for her. This was adorned with small green leaves and petals of lily of the valley. She wafted along like bunting in a breeze.

Of course, she wore the emerald necklace she had bought from Cerys, and had blessed by Queen Una herself. Her fae circlet crowned her lustrous locks which cascaded freely down her back.

Kiera's bouquet contained azaleas which her father grew in the garden of his new house by the sea, which he shared with Zondra. Sunflowers also interspersed the bouquet, along with snowdrops for her mother-in law. And bluebells cascaded over the arrangement. A single bougainvillea had been snuck in by Kiera herself; the flowers had suddenly started growing in Cerys' garden. Her heart was gladdened at the presumed sign that Cerys was happy.

Her attendants gasped at the bride's radiance. Kiera herself, gawped at the beautiful reflection in the mirror. She couldn't quite believe this was all real.

Representatives from Kiera's own Irish and Scottish family clans had journeyed to attend her very special event. As had Heather, Lily and Rose, the witches who had assisted at the start of the quest which was now finding its happy ending.

Ailene had given Kiera the mirror she was staring at, as a gift from her mother's clan. Its frame was gold and harp shaped. A leprechaun had provided the gold for it. It seemed Kiera had captured the attention of many folk during her time in the fae realm.

At moonrise, Kiera was ushered out of her den, where her father waited at her door. She heard a snort, and looked up into the big brown eyes of Roger.

"Oh my, I didn't expect to see you here," she exclaimed.

'Queen Una suggested it, as she was unable to attend,' he told her mind-to-mind.

The unicorn also informed her, *' I am here incognito. Nobody else can see my true form. We wanted to give you our blessings without fuss. This is your day. So don't speak to me out loud.'*

'Oh, OK. Well, thank you for being here.'

'You should probably get on my back now.'

Kiera looked aghast. *' But you are not a horse.'*

'Indeed I am not. Only those I choose are permitted to ride on my back.'

'And you choose me?'

'Yes, but please hurry before people wonder why you're just staring at your 'horse'.'

With a mischievous grin, Kiera kissed his nose.

'Do not push your luck,' he warned her with a shake of his mane.

He couldn't fool her though, she sensed his amusement.

Kiera climbed onto Roger's back, with her father's assistance.

Threaris was glowing with pride as he accompanied his beautiful magickal daughter, walking alongside the 'horse'. She had believed in him when nobody else would, not even himself. She had more strength and power than he ever dreamed possible.

Her power was also evident in the number of couples undergoing the ritual. Only soul matched mated pairs underwent the hand fasting ceremony, and it was only held at this time of year. There were more couples than normal this year.

The whole clan had gathered in a large circle in the sacred space where Kiera had jogged to all those months ago. To the space she'd instinctively known was sacred

It felt like a lifetime had passed since she'd stumbled upon this place. The thought of it being where she'd first met Pryderi brought a smile to her lips as she walked towards the inner circle of males awaiting their brides.

Cerys was officiating, and stood at the head of the inner circle, with Rhion at her side, issuing his approval of the matches.

The brides reached their destination and formed their own circle around the grooms, and a respectful silence descended upon the gathering.

Cerys called the corners to open and protect the sacred space. She then addressed the entire group, declaring the solemnity and importance of the occasion.

Speaking to the couples she announced, " *With full awareness, know that within this circle you are not only declaring your intent to be united before your clan, but also unto the goddess. The promises made here today will bind your souls in an eternal sacred bond. Do you truly wish to proceed?*"

All couples nodded. None would propose the ceremony who were not fully committed and bonded.

" *Uniting couples, I bid you look into each other's eyes. Do you vow to honour and respect one another, and seek only each other's loving arms?*"

" *We will,*" was chorused the couples.

" *Let the first binding be made.*"

Attendants stepped forwards. The couples stood facing each other, and cords were draped right hand to right hand, looped through, and left hand to left hand, securing them in an infinity knot.

Kiera and Pryderi's bond was a pink ribbon, symbolising honour, affection and romance. It honoured their inner animal and all creatures.

"*Where there is pain or struggle, will the other seek to ease these?*" Cerys asked.

"*We will.*"

"*So the second bond is made.*"

Their second bond was unique. They used a long leather cord, to symbolise the one Pryderi used for his prey that they'd had fun with, and which had been used to create Kiera's father's own bond.

"*Where there is happiness will you rejoice, and seek this in your daily lives?*"

"*We will.*"

"*So the third and final bond is made.*"

The attendants stepped forward once more, and tied the final strip around each couples' wrists.

Kiera and Pryderi had selected a gold cord to symbolise the power of their protection, not only to one another but to their clan.

" You are now bound together heart, body and soul in an unbreakable vow. As above so below. May the goddess bless your union with love and light. May you cherish one another always, and provide light in the darkness. For now you are one."

Cheers and applause filled the night air as the couples kissed, sealing their union.

Two attendants waited at the opening of the inner circle, holding a rowan broom. Each couple had to jump over the broom, whilst still tied together by their bonds. It was impossible not to laugh as they leapt.

The couples with their criss-crossed hands led the way happily to the large gathering space. Frydah and Colle had arranged faery lights to light the route.

Cups of nectar wine had been set out on tables. They all took one cup each, except the newlyweds who had to share one precariously between their tied hands.

Rhion raised a toast to the happy unions, and they all took a sip. Pryderi helped hold the cup up to Kiera's mouth first, before she returned the favour. It was a delicate procedure and some wine dribbled down her chin, which Pryderi was all too happy to lick off for her.

The musicians struck up, and the hand fasted couples gathered in a circle to dance. It was a little like a country dance or a ceilidh, but the couples obviously couldn't part. They span in circles, and interwove as they skipped along in their bonded pairs. Utter joy and devotion adorned every face in the dance.

Despite their elinefae vitality, the couples were struggling for breath as the music ended. Dancing and laughing required a lot of energy after the rigours of the ceremony.

The rest of the clan prepared to join the frivolity, awaiting only their musical cue. But Kiera caught Pryderi's cheeky nod to the musicians.

Everyone froze as the first long slow notes blasted out of concealed speakers. The clan were unfamiliar with this sound, and were puzzled and slightly afraid of the howls.

Kiera's hands rose to her mouth, taking Pryderi's with her, as she realised what he'd done. Musical howls echoed as her namesake began to sing 'Whenever Wherever'. Kiera laughed, hoping Pryderi understood just how appropriate his song choice was.

"Cerys showed me how to use your iPod, and I saw your name on there. I like how the song makes me feel," he explained quietly.

Kiera let her hips wiggle in time to the music, feeling slightly frustrated she couldn't fully use her arms. Pryderi was carried along with her.

It didn't take long for the clan to join in and copy her. They thought it was amazing fun, but were still relieved when their own musicians started up for the next song and they could return to their familiar dancing.

'I cannot wait much longer after you wiggled like that,' Pryderi told only her, pulling gently on their bonds to guide her away from the throng.

They made their way awkwardly to their den, still tied together.

"How are we supposed to do this?" Pryderi let out on a breathy laugh, trying to get undressed.

"You have no imagination, husband mine," Kiera sniggered.

She guided their hands to her side, where there were some cords near her underarms. She tugged on one end, and her dress instantly began to loosen.

Pryderi loosened the rest of the ties. With a wriggle of her hips Kiera was free of her garment's confines, and stepped away from the discarded clothing.

Pryderi felt his temperature rise as he went from simmering to boiling hot. His eyes smouldered as he watched his mate disrobe, and felt himself trapped closely to her now naked body.

Kiera looked up with hooded eyes and whispered huskily, "That's me done. Your turn, big boy."

Instead of his usual tight leather trousers Pryderi was wearing loose fitting cotton ones for their big day. Kiera tugged at the elasticated waistband, and helped him jostle out of the clothing, which was a frustrating barrier to where she wanted to be.

Seeing his erection spring free, Kiera panted with desire. She guided them towards the bed and they carefully laid down.

Pryderi's fingers zeroed in on his target. Kiera found herself brushing her own sex along with him, as their fingers explored together. She bit her lip as flames travelled through her core. She heard a deep rumbling growl as her mate lapped at the spots of blood she'd created on her mouth.

Pulling their arms up over their heads Pryderi lunged forwards, entering her in one long smooth thrust as her legs parted to beckon him in.

His tongue delved into her mouth, meeting hers, gliding hungrily, their mouths working furiously.

Not being able to fondle her breasts was frustrating, he wanted to hold onto her, to feel every inch outside as he thrust inside her.

Kiera was struggling against their bonds, also needing the physical contact her hands were used to. She wanted to dig her hands into his back. She wanted to cup his glorious butt cheeks, to draw him in deeper.

The tension built inside both of them as their frustration grew.

Her inner muscles clenched tightly around his cock, as he surged in and out. But it wasn't enough, she needed more.

Her hips bucked to the rhythm he set, making them both moan loudly.

Pryderi suddenly slowed his frantic movements. He let himself still completely, covering her body with his. He was looking deeply into her eyes.

He saw beyond the glow, beyond the colour. He saw through those windows and into her soul. He saw the beauty truly within and was stunned into silence.

Looking back at him, Kiera saw the raw power and beauty inside her mate, making her breath hitch.

With their gazes still locked they sought one another's mouths, but this time the kiss was tender, loving and caring.

"*I love you*," she told him breathily.

"*I love you too*," he murmured.

He sunk his teeth into her shoulder, his love bites harder than they'd ever been before, stinging her as sweetly as she tasted.

Kiera found herself returning the bite, savouring the taste of his blood, sweeter than anything in the fae realm.

The bonds from their wrists dropped away of their own accord.

Licking each other's marks until they healed, Pryderi adjusted his position, and steadied his hand against Kiera's hip. Their united blood was rushing around his entire being, sending his senses reeling.

His other hand was on the side of her head, stroking her hair as he looked longingly into her eyes.

In a low, husky voice he repeated, "*I love you*."

Without waiting for a response he began to move once more, but did not rush.

She felt him sliding with an intensity she'd not felt before. She could hear his heartbeat as if it was hers. It echoed in her ears. Her whole being throbbed with it.

Feeling her shudder below him, he kissed her cheek and checked she was OK. Receiving her positive affirmation, he nipped his way down her neck.

His long drawn out strokes were making both of them tremble.

Their cheeks rubbed together as he drew himself up and down her body.

Their scents were mingling thickly in the air all around them.

He could resist no longer, and kissed along her neck down to her shoulder, his hips moving with gathering force.

In turn, she nuzzled into his neck, whilst reaching her hand around to the back of his head, her fingers combing through his hair.

Her mouth sucked along his shoulder. His body increased its speed in response.

In unison, they bit into the shoulder their teeth had found.

Fireworks burst behind their eyes as the sting and blood hit their senses at once.

They roared with passion, and their hips drove together with an explosion of energy.

Kiera arched her back and her head was thrown back as her orgasm exploded through her, making her scream out in sweet agonising bliss.

Pryderi was roaring his own release as he was driven by the madness of his need.

Their bodies were still moving and colliding, travelling through the darkness to join their light. Their joint orgasm continued to thrust them together in every way possible for five minutes.

Finally they stilled to catch their breath before Pryderi rolled to his side, gathering his mate to him.

Kiera rested her head on his firm chest, feeling replete. She felt and heard his deep satisfied breath as he blew out in wonderment.

"That was intense," she whispered.

"Hmmm..." he hummed in agreement.

Kissing the top of her head he regretfully added, "But we should be getting back before we're missed too much."

"What? No. Can't we stay here?"

"Apologies, my love. We go or we will be fetched."

She could have happily stayed in their bed, intertwined forever, but she forced herself up to leave.

Pryderi helped her back into her dress, fighting the urge to play with her body and drag her back to bed all the while.

Shrugging his own trousers back on, he sighed his own regret.

Kiera righted her hair and makeup quickly.

With a quick kiss, the pair departed arm-in-arm back into the night to rejoin the party with their clan.

A fine mist of rain was falling and their path was illuminated by a moonbow. With a flutter, three silhouetted birds flew through it, disappearing into the distance.

———

Glossary of Names

Name	Pronunciation
Ailene	a-*lean*
Althea	*ael-thEE-uh*
Arwyn	*aar-wihn*
Azalea	*uh-z-ai-lee-uh*
Cailean	*kay-lun*
Cerys	*keh-rihs*
Colle	*kohl*
Donnagan	*don-uhg-un*
Dougal	*do-gawl*
Eileithyia	*eel-eeth-EE-aa*
Eirlys	*ayr-lihs*
Elan	*ee-lan*
Elinefae	*ee-LINE-fay*
Frydah	*free-dah*
Kiera	*key-air-uh*
Pryderi	*pruh-DAIR-ee*
Rhion	*ree-on*
Roarke	*rawrk*
Shakira	*shu-KEER-uh*
Shui	*shw-aay*
Sinead	*shin-ade*
Terrah	*tehr-rahr*
Threaris	*three-AH-is*
Una	*oo-nah*
Zondra	*zon-drah*

About the Author

TL Clark is a British author who stumbles through life as if it were a gauntlet of catastrophes.

Rather than playing the victim she uses these unfortunate events to fuel her passion for writing, for reaching out to help others.

Her dream is to buy a farmhouse, so she can run a retreat for those who are feeling frazzled by the stresses of the modern world.

She writes about different kinds of love in the hope that she'll uncover its mysteries.

Her loving husband (and very spoiled cat) have proven to her that true love really does exist.
Writing has shown her that coffee may well be the source of life.

If you would like to follow TL or just drop in for a chat online, @tlclarkauthor will find her across most social media:

Instagram, Facebook, Goodreads, Twitter…

She also has a **blog** where she shares random thoughts and book reviews. She's very kind and supportive, so often reviews other indie authors.

You can also sign up for her newsletter on her blog, to ensure you don't miss any exciting news (about new releases or special offers).

www.tlclarkauthor.blogspot.co.uk

Other books by TL Clark

<u>Young's Love</u> – Striving for independence and finding gelato in Tuscany.

A gentle journey that explores Samantha's cry for freedom. She has an unhappy, controlled marriage which just keeps getting worse.

At breaking point, she goes on a couples' holiday to Tuscany. As she finds independence can she also find love? Can she become the woman she always wanted to be?

<u>Trues Love</u> – Suspense and suspended reality in Ibiza.

Amanda Trueman loves her single, wild and carefree lifestyle. Read about her erotic adventures in this rollercoaster of a book.

She heads off with her best friend to the sunny skies of Ibiza for a holiday which promises to supply even more fun memories.

A blonde bombshell certainly fits the bill, but he soon has her heart exposed as well as her flesh.

Feeling vulnerable, will Amanda sink or swim in the world of true love? Danger lurks. Is their relationship doomed to end in disaster?

<u>Dark Love</u> – A romance novel with BDSM in it too.

This book follows Jonathan, a male Submissive. His attention is grabbed by another woman, but can he bear to turn his back on the life he's always known and loved? Is it even possible?

This book investigates the love that exists in a BDSM relationship and beyond.

<u>Broken & Damaged Love</u> – a book with an important message.

This one comes with a trigger warning, as it features a sexually abused girl.

It was written to give hope to CSA survivors. They too can go on to have healthy, happy relationships.

It also aims to help others watch out for signs, so they can help stop abuse.

Profits are regularly donated to charity from the sale of this book.

<u>Rekindled Love</u> – Hatches, matches and dispatches.

We join Sophie just in time for her first 'experience', but she gets torn away from her first love.

We go on to follow her life, through marriage, birth and death. Hers is not an easy life, but hold her hand through the bumpy bits to get to the good times.

There's a rollercoaster of emotions waiting for you.

That's all for now.

Thank you for reading. Don't forget to post a quick review.

Love and light,

TL Clark

Lightning Source UK Ltd.
Milton Keynes UK
UKHW040212020519

341979UK00001B/1/P